D0840143

SPECIAL MESSAGE TO READERS

THE ULVERSCROFT FOUNDATION
(registered UK charity number 264873)

was established in 1972 to provide funds for
research, diagnosis and treatment of eye diseases.
Examples of major projects funded by
the Ulverscroft Foundation are:-

- The Children's Eye Unit at Moorfields Eye Hospital, London
- The Ulverscroft Children's Eye Unit at Great Ormond Street Hospital for Sick Children
- Funding research into eye diseases and treatment at the Department of Ophthalmology, University of Leicester
- The Ulverscroft Vision Research Group, Institute of Child Health
- Twin operating theatres at the Western Ophthalmic Hospital, London
- The Chair of Ophthalmology at the Royal Australian College of Ophthalmologists

You can help further the work of the Foundation
by making a donation or leaving a legacy.
Every contribution is gratefully received. If you
would like to help support the Foundation or
require further information, please contact:

THE ULVERSCROFT FOUNDATION
The Green, Bradgate Road, Anstey
Leicester LE7 7FU, England
Tel: (0116) 236 4325

website: www.foundation.ulverscroft.com

DERBY JOHN'S ALIBI

Derby John Daggert is out for revenge on his employer after a severe beating meted out for theft and adultery. Then a robbery goes badly wrong, two men are murdered, and the killer makes a wild ride from Querida to Denver. As prime suspect, Daggert is arrested, but his lawyer convinces the jury he was elsewhere when the crime was committed. It is left to Buckskin Joe Swann to hunt down the culprit — a task more difficult than he could have ever imagined . . .

ETHAN FLAGG

DERBY JOHN'S ALIBI

Complete and Unabridged

LINFORD
Leicester

First published in Great Britain in 2014 by
Robert Hale Limited
London

First Linford Edition
published 2016
by arrangement with
Robert Hale
an imprint of The Crowood Press
Wiltshire

A catalogue record for this book is available
from the British Library.

ISBN 978–1–4448–2969–3

Published by
F. A. Thorpe (Publishing)
Anstey, Leicestershire
Set by Words & Graphics Ltd.
Anstey, Leicestershire
Printed and bound in Great Britain by
T. J. International Ltd., Padstow, Cornwall

This book is printed on acid-free paper

1

Sticky Fingers

An angry snarl twisted the man's face as he studied the whiskey bottle in his right hand. Wearing a sour expression, he tipped the dwindling contents into a glass. The cigar clutched tightly between his teeth had long since died.

For most of that day he had been seated at the rear of the Laughing Coyote saloon in the southern Colorado town of Alamosa. Customers had come and gone. Yet still the man remained, nursing this, his second bottle of hard liquor.

Not a word had passed his lips since ordering that first bottle. Nobody had liked to interrupt the solitary drinker. It was clear that he had something serious on his mind. Something that did not merit any curious enquiry. Such an act was unlikely to be received with good grace.

Happy Jack Tranter, the bartender and owner of the Laughing Coyote, was displaying something less than his customary jovial demeanour. Like all good barmen, he could read the signs of impending discord from a distance. His pudgy snout wrinkled. This guy smelled rank. And not only from an unwashed viewpoint.

He exuded bad trouble. A simmering volcano that could erupt at any moment. Even the house cat, a skinny ginger tom employed to keep the rodent population at bay, gave him a wide berth.

Tranter signalled to his partner that he was going over to speak to the lone drinker. The response was a cautionary grimace. Ike Barlow had also sensed the mood of impending discord.

'Play it cool, Jack,' advised his partner. 'Fellas like that don't take kindly to being disturbed.'

Tranter nodded and sidled over to the table. The barman stood facing the slovenly-dressed character. Again, he couldn't help sniffing aloud at the odorous specimen. His presence was ignored as the man continued staring into the bottom of his glass.

The bartender coughed. It emerged more as a nervous croak. His jaunty air had dissolved along with the whiskey in the guy's glass.

The drinker slowly lifted his head. A sardonic eye matched the sneer of disdain that greeted this unwelcome disturbance.

'You want some'n, mister?' the surly customer spat out.

The terse rejoinder emerged as a slurred drawl. It was clear that the whiskey was hard at work on the guy's soused brain. Also evident was the scruffy personal appearance. Here was a man who had abandoned the social niceties of deportment. His black hair was unkempt and greasy. A ten-days' growth of beard cloaked the angular face, in which were entwined the remnants of his last meal.

Only one item stood out from the wretched human mess. A shiny well-cared-for Remington six-shooter was stuck in his shellbelt. This made the guy dangerous. Happy Jack knew that he had to tread carefully.

'I was just w-wondering if'n you intended taking a r-room for the night?' stammered the barman, struggling to maintain a weak grin. 'We got clean beds and a complementary bathtub out back.' A droplet of sweat trickled down the barman's shiny bald pate and dripped on to the table.

The man slammed a fist down on the green baize. The whiskey bottle teetered, then tipped over, spilling the dregs across the felt cloth.

'You suggesting I need a bath?' he snarled.

'N-no, of course not, sir,' Tranter hurried on, forcing his mouth to register another unctuous smile. 'Just a friendly enquiry, is all.'

The man huffed. His bleary eyes settled on the empty bottle. 'Now look what you've gone and made me do. Clumsy damned beertapper.' His right hand strayed to the gun butt.

The blood drained from Tranter's round face.

'I'll get you another, sir. On the house.'

Now that was more like it. Free booze. A leery grin split the drinker's blotched cheeks.

'Then hurry it up!' he snapped.

With his glass topped up by the fresh bottle, Johnny Daggert once again sank into a lethargic state of sullen bitterness.

How had he come to be in this sorry state?

From being the pride of the Kentucky horse racing fraternity, he was now a washed-out drunk who could barely afford the price of a bottle of cheap booze. His pockets were all but empty.

A sigh of regret hissed from somewhere beneath the frazzled beard as he cast his thoughts back to the time when his name was spoken of with awe and respect.

Yes, indeed, mused the morose toper. Those were the days.

Known statewide as Derby John, he had earned the prestigious nickname by winning the famed Kentucky Derby two years on the run. The jockey had been fêted and wooed by the top echelons of the racing world. Life was a dream come true. He had his pick of all the best restaurants in Louisville. But more exciting for a virile man about town was that women literally threw themselves at the debonair celebrity.

He took to wearing the small round hat made fashionable by the women who attended the race meetings. Once the renowned jockey began wearing the headgear, it rapidly became a male accessory as well. The name of Derby John Daggert was soon on everybody's lips.

The gravy train was well and truly running at full speed.

Then, almost overnight, everything had suddenly changed.

Daggert had become jealous when another horse threatened to take away his crown. In retaliation, he attempted to nobble the challenger on the night before the big race. Fortune had abruptly ceased to smile upon him when he was caught red-handed administering a potent drug.

To avoid the disgrace and ignominy of being exposed in public, Johnny had immediately fled the state and headed west.

That had been two years before.

When he reached Colorado it was clear that the mining industry was in full swing. Discoveries of gold and silver were being registered almost every day. This was a place for a man to make his mark.

But striking paydirt was haphazard and involved back-breaking toil. And Johnny Daggert was lazy by nature. He was loath to overly exert himself. Physical labour was not for him. There had to be other easier and more lucrative ways of creaming off the wealth being generated in the gold camps.

Being an ex-jockey, gambling was in his blood. So he naturally gravitated towards the green baize tables. And, while the paydirt lasted, a never-ending supply of gullible prospectors flocked to the numerous boom towns that grew up overnight. All were eager and willing to spend their loot in the many saloons catering to their every whim.

When he arrived in the booming township of Cripple Creek, his mind was made up. He would set himself up as a gambler.

But horse racing and cards are completely different sides of the same coin. Poker is a game that demands patience and nerve. To begin with he played with miners, who were easy to dupe. But Johnny soon grew impatient with the low returns. He became greedy, began pushing his luck and soon found that he lacked the necessary acumen for high-stakes ventures. Impulsive and rash in his betting, he began to lose more and more.

When his meagre funds ran low, the chiseller resorted to fraud. Discovery was the inevitable result of his inept handling of the cards. The furore that erupted led to him being run out of town on a rail.

But Daggert was not a man to lie

down and accept such a public humiliation.

That night he stole some lamp oil and poured it over the array of tents that made up much of the growing settlement. A match was struck and applied to the outermost structure. Then he quickly disappeared into the gloom. From a low knoll above Cripple Creek, the fireman watched the camp quickly succumb to the flames. A wolfish grin split the arsonist's features as he chuckled gleefully, well satisfied with his vengeful deed.

'Nobody gets the better of Derby John,' he muttered as panic-stricken shouts for help elicited a further bout of buoyant guffawing. But this was not the time for loitering in the vicinity of the growing conflagration.

Drifting south through numerous mining camps boasting colourful names such as Tin Cup, Gothic, Quartz and Turret, he finally arrived in Querida. The town had grown up on the banks of Grape Creek following a large gold strike. Johnny managed to secure a job working for one of the main assay agents in the territory.

It didn't pay overly well, but was OK while he bided his time. Then the inevitable happened. Once again, he overstepped the mark.

Another slug of hard liquor coursed down his gullet. The much abused passageway was now immune to the fiery assault as the whole sorry episode lurched back into focus. A spasm of pain rippled across his back on recollection of the grim events that had led to his current situation.

It had taken place three weeks before. The fiery tipple did nought to assuage the anger that flooded his being. Derby John was once again thinking about retribution. But on this occasion it was the strutting figure of Frisco De Vere who was going to pay a heavy price.

* * *

The morning was bright. It was going to be another hot one. Sun streamed in through an open window. Johnny Daggert rolled up his shirtsleeves. He was working on the assay ledgers. The large heavy books contained lists of all the mining transactions accepted by the firm of De Vere Holdings.

Frisco De Vere was the boss. A dour, rather stuffy man in his mid-forties, he was nevertheless an astute entrepreneur who also owned half a dozen gold mines up in the San Isabel Mountains.

De Vere considered himself to be a shrewd judge of men. That trait had come to the fore when he had hired Johnny Daggert to handle the books. Business was booming and De Vere needed somebody he could trust, not having the time to allocate such a delicate task to himself.

So when Johnny Daggert had wandered in off the street, looking for work, De Vere had seen beyond the guy's downtrodden appearance. He had instantly recognized his potential as a useful hand. The newcomer was signed up on the spot.

It had not taken Daggert long to

prove his worth. He was smart and had the learning. Figures came easily to him — the result of calculating odds on the race tracks of Kentucky. As a result he was soon given the responsibility of managing all the company paperwork.

What the boss had failed to suss out, however, was his new employee's wily propensity for self-aggrandisement.

One of Daggert's tasks was to check and store the large amounts of gold and silver that passed through the assay office. This only served to resurrect the ex-jockey's glossy image of the high life that he had once enjoyed as a matter of course. Achieving the pre-eminent position of top racing man in Kentucky had brought untold wealth to the farm boy from Virginia.

But maintaining the lifestyle at the upper end of society came at a price. The money had quickly disappeared. Then along came that other darned nag to challenge the pre-eminence of his own revered arab stallion, Black Shadow.

The green-eyed dragon was soon leaning over Johnny's shoulder, whispering lurid thoughts that he found impossible to resist. Not that he had any wish to. Soon, the new clerk began skimming off small amounts of gold dust into his own secret account. Nothing too obvious that would arouse suspicion.

On this particular morning, the sly clerk was working alongside an old has-been called Israel Swann. Being a retired miner, Swann was well versed in the intricacies of measuring ore content. The jasper had become too old for the heavy work at the Bonanza mine up in the hills above Querida.

De Vere, considering himself to be a benevolent employer, had put Israel in charge of assaying the ore content brought in by prospectors. Once it had been analysed and weighed by his ageing colleague, Daggert then did all the administrative work. Booking in the amounts and issuing receipts was beyond the old dude's ability.

The new guy despised Swann on account of his learning deficiency. Unfortunately for Daggert, he had sadly underestimated his ageing colleague. Swann might have won and lost two fortunes but his loyalty to De Vere for not ditching him was rock solid.

Unlike his boss, old Israel could spot a charlatan at 1,000 paces. Almost from the beginning he had caught on to his devious associate's underhand practice.

The old-timer was placed in a quandary. Not a snitch by habit, he hoped that Daggert's sticky fingers were just a temporary aberration. A slight divergence from an honest trail. So nothing was done. Israel was well aware that his boss was ruthless when it came to dealing with wayward employees.

There was that time when Janus Blacktop, the manager up at the Tomboy Mine, was caught paying himself extra wages for work that had not been undertaken. Blacktop had suddenly disappeared, never to be seen again. Rumours circulated as to his fate, none of them pleasant.

2

Femme Fatale

On this particular morning, Derby John was engaged in his normal tasks when the street door of the office opened. In walked a well-dressed woman. Daggert's eyes bulged wide. She was definitely not one of the usual clientele they were accustomed to serving. Rough-and-tumble prospectors couldn't hold a candle to this dame.

She was a good ten years older than he, but no less of a stunner for that. Age had been kind to the delectable peach. She seemed to float across the floor like a leaf on the breeze.

Unlike most of the women he had encountered in the tough frontier townships of Colorado, she exuded an aura of sophistication and mystery that was far more in keeping with the women he had known back in Louisville.

''Morning, Mrs De Vere,' Israel Swann quickly greeted the vision of beauty. Removing his battered hat, the old guy gave the visitor a fawning bow. 'We ain't had the pleasure of seeing you in here for a spell.'

Letitia De Vere received the salutation with an aloof nod while slowly adjusting the natty hat perched on her mass of red tresses. All the while her probing gaze was focused on the latest employee. Casually she swung a frilly parasol while casting a contemplative eye over the tall stranger.

A slight twist of the rouge lips indicated that the verdict was in the affirmative.

'I don't recall having the pleasure,' she purred, holding out a gloved hand. The last word was delivered in a more than suggestive manner.

'That is certainly my loss, Mrs De Vere,' replied Daggert, holding the woman's seductive stare.

He quickly adjusted the black derby

to a jaunty angle before accepting the proffered appendage. He held on to the slim hand rather longer than was necessary. The glittering smile of an experienced lothario enhanced the touch of rouge on the woman's smooth cheeks. All the social graces of sweet talk and flattery, long since packed away, were quickly revived. After stepping around the counter, Johnny indicated for the woman to accompany him.

Old Israel was quickly forgotten.

'But now that you have deigned to pay us a visit, perhaps I could show you some of the improvements that have been made since your husband so kindly took me into his employ.'

Letitia tipped her head in acknowledgement and followed him through to the back office. Swann was left to twiddle his fingers. A simmering resentment had been unknowingly fostered.

From that day onward the boss's wife became a frequent visitor to the office. Those citizens of a more curious disposition might have noticed that old Israel was absent during most of these visitations. Derby John's devious plan of seduction was being conducted with military precision.

Soon he was visiting the lady's home. Within weeks he was firmly ensconced in her bed.

Johnny's disdain for his old associate had been ill-judged. Swann was no slow-witted dupe. He had quickly cottoned on to the fact that his younger colleague was playing with fire. Thinking it might just be an innocent friendship, once again he held fire over any action. But with gold still going missing, his patience was wearing thin.

Mrs De Vere had strayed from the matrimonial path before. There was that land speculator from Wyoming, the cattle buyer from Dodge City and a passing snake-oil salesman. All had dallied awhile but soon passed on their way. The assignations had been brief and without any substance. So Israel had held his tongue.

John Daggert was becoming a permanent fixture. That made him far more of a threat to the boss's well-being. Only when the deceiving duo shifted their affair to the matrimonial home while De Vere was away on business did Swann feel it necessary to expose the duplicity.

Frisco De Vere had been good to Israel. Most employers would have just kicked out those who could no longer pull their weight. De Vere had given him a job in the office and allowed him to remain in a company cabin rent free. Israel reckoned he owed him.

Exposing the duplicity of a scurrilous thief and dandy could not go unchallenged. He placed the blame firmly on the head of Derby John Daggart, convincing himself that the boss's wife had been lured into the honey-trap by the smooth-talking charmer.

The crunch arrived one night. De Vere was supposedly away for a couple of days on business in Salida. Letitia had arranged for her lover to come round to the house after dark. Making certain that no prying neighbours were in sight, Daggert slipped in through the back door.

Letitia immediately fell into his arms. They kissed with a wild passion of abandonment. The woman was insatiable. She couldn't wait to get him upstairs. Daggert almost felt sorry for his boss. But not enough to temper his own innate urges.

'You do love me, don't you, Johnny?' she whispered in that husky voice that always set him all aquiver. 'Frisco is nowhere near the man you are.'

'Of course I do,' he replied automatically. It was always the same with these dames. All they seemed to want was to fall in love. Yet all Johnny Daggert wanted was a good time with no strings attached.

The problem was that Letitia was becoming rather too pressing. The bedroom department he could handle. It was her recent suggestions that their liaison should be placed on a more permanent footing that disturbed him. Maybe it was time to call time on this particular affiliation.

The woman had picked up on his hesitant mood.

'Is something the matter, my darling?' she murmured, stroking his wavy black locks and nestling further into his embrace. 'You seem a little preoccupied tonight.'

Johnny was given no time to respond.

Suddenly his world came tumbling down as the bedroom door crashed back on its hinges. Four men rushed into the room, each toting a six-shooter. They were led by De Vere.

'Get that bastard out of my bed,' the mine-owner snarled with barely contained fury. Three of the men lunged at the startled lothario, dragging him out. He was completely naked. The men sniggered. But De Vere was in no mood for levity.

Threatening glowers quickly removed the smirking expressions.

Letitia screamed, cowering back into the bedclothes.

De Vere jabbed a finger at her. 'I'll deal with you later,' he ranted, his face purple with unsuppressed rage. 'But first I need to teach this piece of dirt a lesson he'll never forget.'

He threw the unfortunate trickster's clothes at him. With no chance to utter anything other than startled grunts, Daggert was hustled down the back stairs and outside. He barely had time to scramble into his trousers and shirt when he was heaved on to his horse. Rough hands tied him face down on the saddle. Any cries for help were shut off by a grubby bandanna gag.

Just before the moon's silvery glow disappeared, he noticed a figure disappearing round the corner of the house. That shambling limp was unmistakable.

Israel Swann.

The bastard had shopped him. Even through his fear of the immediate future, Daggert made himself a promise. If he came through this dire predicament, that old snake would pay for his betrayal.

But for now he could only trust that somehow he would survive De Vere's wrath.

A grimace twisted the captive's tight features as the ropes bit deep into his limbs. These guys knew exactly what they were doing. They had been well briefed following Swann's revelation of his colleague's lecherous actions. To complete the process of disorientation, a flour sack was jammed over his head.

The old-timer watched as the group of riders headed off into the night. He was not smiling. His face remained tight-lipped. Knowing what he had unleashed gave the informant some cause for doubting the wisdom of his course of action.

If his nemesis had any say in the matter, he would come to regret his actions.

But for the moment, Daggert could do nothing except curse his own stupidity. *Never bite the hand that feeds you* was a maxim that he ought to have heeded. Too late for that now.

The riders galloped onward for what seemed like a bunch of lifetimes to the captive. In effect it was little more than thirty minutes later when a muffled voice called a halt.

'Get him off the horse and tied to that tree.'

De Vere was in no mood for soft talk. The crack of a whip tore apart the silence. Daggert's heart missed a beat. He knew what was coming. Janus Blacktop's mysterious fate had spread throughout the De Vere enterprise. The bullwhip had played no small part in the reports.

A coyote howled a sad lament somewhere out in the darkness.

Blood thundered inside Daggert's head from the severe jolting of the night ride. Gasps for air matched the terror now weighing heavily on his guilty conscience.

Suddenly a dense silence once again enfolded the clearing at the end of the blind draw. Daggert tried to look round but he was effectively pinioned to the trunk of a cottonwood. None of his assailants had uttered a word since leaving the De Vere house. He tried ineffectually to control his hammering chest.

Then suddenly, the shirt was ripped off his back.

He sucked in a deep breath, waiting. Blood dribbled down his chin where he had bitten his lip. He stiffened, ready to take his punishment. If nothing else, Derby John did not lack for courage.

A low voice barely above a whisper penetrated the mush of his brain.

'Nobody makes a mug of Frisco De Vere,' growled the menacing cadence. 'Those that do pay a heavy price, as you are about to discover. And it's gonna be a double dose of medicine administered by my friend here.' The whip cracked.

He was referring to the stolen gold dust as well as the violation of his wife. The victim was now fully aware that Israel Swann had known all along about his sticky fingers. An agonizing wait lasting mere seconds was followed by a hiss like steam escaping from a kettle. It was the first intimation that the brutal treatment had begun.

No opportunity to express his regret was given as the deadly brown coil snaked across the exposed shoulders.

The sudden shock of plaited leather on bare flesh knocked the breath from Daggert's body. He did not cry out, so intense was the ripping pain.

The next strike was like being hit by a charging bull. At that moment, the true nature of his torment sunk in. A tortured scream rent the air. Three more brutally administered blows followed. And only then did the torment pause as Frisco De Vere deigned to address his victim again.

The voice was calm and measured in its delivery.

'This is what skunks and varmints can expect when they steal from me. And you, *Mister* Daggert, have excelled in your greed in more ways than one.'

De Vere nodded to one of his men, a hulking bear named Grizzly Jones. The tough flexed his muscular arms and flicked the lethal serpent out to its full length before resuming the pitiless chastisement.

3

Buckskin Joe

A young man was busily engaged outside his log cabin, 200 miles to the north. Located some two miles from Fort Fetterman in Wyoming territory, it was home to Buckskin Joe Swann. The army scout had made the choice to live in this isolated clearing in the shadow of the Laramie Mountains in preference to the bustling confinement of the military enclave.

Joe valued his privacy. Being a civilian, he was not subject to army regulations in his free time. The scout was also a proficient hunter, favouring homemade clothes fashioned from the creatures of the forests: deerskin breeches and a fringed jacket. The long boots were of more robust elk hide. His only concession to so-called civilized apparel was a wide-brimmed plainsman hat.

The jacket had been discarded to reveal rippling cords of muscle on the naked torso as he hefted an axe. The blade fell to cleave asunder another log. Joe enjoyed the strain of physical work. Sweat glistened on the well-toned body. The early spring sun was more than welcome after the hard winter.

An expert with the longbow, the scout had been taught how to use it by Dark Cloud, chief of the eastern Arapahoe. That was before the Indians rebelled against the relentless encroachment of white settlers on to their tribal lands.

Equally practised was Joe's skill with the six-shooter and Winchester rifle. Setting the axe aside, he now took hold of the rifle. His discerning eye had picked out a movement on the far side of the level plateau. The long gun was always kept close by. Predators of both the animal and human kind were never far away.

Joe had established a rapport with the Indian tribes. But the constant influx of white settlers from the East had made for a tense and highly volatile situation in the territory. Being an army scout had made him an automatic enemy of the red man. Under such circumstances, friendship was an unpredictable ally that could flicker and die at the drop of a hat.

He squinted into the morning sunlight.

A rider was heading his way. When the visitor was halfway across the grassy sward, Joe recognized the upright figure of Leif Erickson. Long blond locks trailed behind the galloping horseman like a ripe field of corn. The Swede had been an army scout before leaving to join the burgeoning US Mail department.

Joe had been happy to take over his duties.

The dark-blue jacket and peaked cap were a dead giveaway. Leif must have a letter to deliver. Discarding the rifle, Joe used an old flannel shirt to wipe the sweat from his glistening torso. Most likely it was from his father. Israel Swann was an ore prospector of the old school. Ever since the discovery of gold in California he had been drawn to the next big strike like a bee to the honeypot.

Only after Joe was born did Israel and his wife settle down to the mundane task of dirt farming. Jenny Swann had succumbed to a smallpox epidemic when Joe was only twelve. Thereafter, he was raised by his father until such time as the old boy reckoned the lad could manage alone. Then Israel had headed off to Nevada to investigate yet another strike.

But Israel always kept in touch with his son. Sometimes it might be a year before a letter was received. When one did eventually arrive, it often contained a sepia-tinted photo of the old boy taken in some far-off picture gallery. If Israel had struck it rich, some paper money was also included.

On this occasion it had been six months since the last contact.

The messenger hurtled at full pelt towards Joe. Only at the very last minute did he haul back on the leathers, skidding to a halt no more than a foot from the unconcerned recipient.

Erikson grinned down at his old buddy.

'One of these days I scare pants off you, Joe Swann, and make you move.'

'Think you can frighten me?' Joe grinned. 'Not a chance.' Then it was down to the nitty gritty. 'You got a letter for me?'

The mailman delved into his leather satchel, pulled out the missive and handed it over. 'Looks like your pa's writing,' said Erikson.

Joe shook his head. 'Pa ain't had the schooling. He always gets someone else to write his letters.' He slipped the rare delivery into the pocket of his buckskin jacket. 'I'll read it this evening. Why don't you step down and have a drink? I've just bottled up some fresh elderberry moonshine.'

The messenger leapt off his lathered

mount. 'If'n is anything like last batch, I'd best limit to a couple of glasses. That stuff made me fall off my horse.'

Joe laughed. 'I bet that was a sight to see.' He slung an arm round his friend's shoulder as they walked over to the cabin.

Later that evening, when the sun was setting over the Laramie Hills, Joe opened the letter. It contained the usual outline of what his father had been up to over the last few months. The main item of interest was that age had finally caught up with the old boy.

Israel had been forced to retire from the Bonanza mine where he had been working for the last two years. But his employer had sympathized with the old man's plight and given him a job in the assay office. Joe gave the benevolent gesture a nod of approval. Most owners would have shrugged off the guy's plight as not their concern.

It appeared that the feisty old buck had landed on his feet there.

The letter went on to add that another

guy had come to work in the office doing the paperwork. But there was something about him that Israel did not trust. Nothing more was said about that issue.

Joe frowned. What could have prompted such a negative assessment? His father was usually so positive about most people he mentioned.

Israel finished by stating that he hoped they could meet up in the near future, maybe in Denver when the boss went to look over some new equipment for the mine. He often took Israel along, valuing his father's expertise in that area.

Sounds good to me, mused Joe, pouring himself another slug of hooch. After his session with Leif Erickson Joe knew he would sleep well that night. But the intimation that something was not quite right with his father kept filtering into his sleepy brain. He finally drifted off in the early hours.

It was lucky that the following day was a Sunday, the day of rest. He would need it. The colonel had delegated him to scout the valley of the Medicine Bow for signs of hostile Indian activity. Thoughts concerning his father's mysterious new colleague were swept into a corner whilst he nursed a mammoth hangover. That latest batch of hooch sure packed a mighty wallop.

Once the man inside his head had ceased his hammering, Joe Swann read his father's letter for a second time. It was a habit that he always followed. Somehow it brought him closer to the old guy. Even though it wasn't him writing the missive, they certainly were Israel Swann's words. By closing his eyes Joe could imagine his pa sitting opposite, talking just like they had always done when he was a young sprout itching to make his mark on the world.

The notion that Joe's father might have uncovered some skulduggery did not cause the young army scout any concern. He knew that the elder Swann was a cautious jasper and wouldn't needlessly place himself in jeopardy.

Little did Buckskin Joe realize that his kinsman would blunder into a hornet's nest from which there was no escape.

* * *

A loud cawing roused the supine man from his comatose state.

Johnny Daggert shifted his tortured frame. A jolt of agony lanced across the dozen bloody wheals scarring his back. He was lying on the ground. It occurred to his dazed brain that sometime during the night he must have slipped off his horse. Forcing open a bleary eye, he perceived an ugly beaked head.

A buzzard. And the darned creature was eyeing him up for its next meal.

Staggering to his feet, the pain-racked frame hollered and waved its arms. The bird recognized that on this occasion it was to be denied. Large flapping wings lifted the heavy body into the azure firmament.

By a stroke of good fortune, or perhaps it was his horse pulling up suddenly, Daggert had come to rest beside a small creek. Gently he lowered himself into the cooling liquid. The chilled wash served to anaesthetize the stinging agony from his recent torment.

He lay there until the cold made him shiver. Dragging himself out of the water, he lurched to his feet. The faithful stallion was chewing on a clump of gramma grass near by. Daggert could see that his saddle-bags were still draped across the cantle.

But had they been tampered with?

With bated breath he moved across to the animal and delved inside the bags. Nothing appeared to have been removed. His tormentors must have been too wrapped up in completing their punitive task to search his belongings.

Further probing in the bag elicited another deep sigh of relief, accompanied by a caustic laugh. Daggert bent double as he howled with glee. Two prairie dogs pricked up their tiny ears. What was this crazy intruder doing in their domain?

'How about that, you critters?' he yelled at the startled animals.

The truth was that De Vere had failed to appreciate that his stolen gold was sitting right under his nose. Not only that, Daggert now had a clean shirt with which to cover his badly mutilated body. Far more important, however, was that his Remington cartridge pistol and shell belt had not been discovered. Now he had the means to survive. In the other bag were some old sticks of beef jerky. Tough and barely edible, they would keep him going until such time as he reached the next town.

Two days later the injured man came across a mission station run by the Sisters of Mercy. Asking no questions as to the origin of his injuries, the nuns tended him until he was fit enough to travel. No payment was expected for the treatment. But Johnny Daggert was grateful for their ministrations and handed over some of his accumulated store of gold.

Ten days later he found himself in the town of Alamosa nursing a glass of whiskey in the Laughing Coyote saloon. He was lucky to be here. All hope of reaching civilization following his departure from the remote mission had been abandoned. Losing his way amidst the arid wasteland of the Crestone sand dunes had almost finished the job that De Vere had started.

Jicarillo Apaches were known to roam across this bleak terrain. The tribe had named the dunes *Sei-anyedi*, which means 'it goes up and down'. Daggert could certainly concur with the Indian philosophy.

On one occasion he had almost blundered into a small hunting party. Luckily Black Shadow had sniffed out the alien presence of Indian ponies. A snicker of alarm warned his boss just in time. Daggert pulled off the trail to conceal himself behind a cluster of rocks. Five minutes later the Indians passed by no more than a stone's throw distant. The concealed man held his breath and, thankfully, they did not sense his presence.

Nonetheless, he waited for a good

hour before continuing his journey.

Mile after gruelling mile of never-ending sandy waves followed. Nothing could grow in such a bleak wilderness. He could only marvel at how the Apache seemed to thrive under such conditions.

After that he had plodded onward until sand surrendered at last to grassland. Only the resilience of his trusty thoroughbred stallion had seen him through the grim ordeal. With safety assured, he had promised the animal the finest attention at the first settlement they encountered.

'I sure owe you that, fella,' he muttered to the patrician black head, tweaking its ears, 'for bringing me out of that darned cauldron.'

The animal snickered in agreement.

4

Robbery

Alamosa had grown up on the banks of the mighty Rio Grande where the Rocky Mountains had surrendered to rolling plains. At this point the river narrowed sufficiently to enable it to be crossed. As a result, it had become the focus of traffic from all points of the compass.

At that moment the bright sunlight filtering through the saloon's grimy windows was cut off. A man had approached the table. The drinker stiffened. What did that fat jigger of barman want now?

'You again, mister?' snapped Daggert without looking up. 'Can't a guy have no peace in this fleapit?'

'You got me all wrong, fella,' protested the newcomer, injecting a mild guffaw into the remark to allay any violent reaction. 'I'm just enquiring after the owner of the arab stallion outside.' The speaker was a tall dude dressed in a black suit. 'The barman said it belonged to you.'

Daggert pushed his hat back. A pair of whiskey-sozzled eyes peered up at the stranger.

'What business is that of your'n?'

'I'd be willing to give you a good price,' replied the man, undeterred by the drinker's belligerent manner. 'Ain't seen a finer piece of horseflesh this side of the Pecos. That animal could make Albuquerque in a day and not draw sweat.'

Daggert presented him with a dour expression before returning his attention to the whiskey bottle. 'He ain't for sale. Now beat it!'

The man stood his ground. 'Name your price, mister,' the trader persisted. He was totally blind to the angry sidewinder he was bugging. 'I'll match it dollar for dollar.'

The saloon had fallen silent as the patrons sensed an imminent eruption. They did not have long to wait. A growl rumbled in the drinker's throat. Bubbling up from deep within, it culminated in Daggert lurching to his feet. His chair fell back as his right hand palmed the Remington in one easy motion. Drink might have made him bellicose, but it sure hadn't affected his reflexes.

'When I say he ain't for sale, that's exactly what I mean,' snarled the glowering man. 'Now heave your mangy carcass out of here afore I give it an airing.' A couple of shots pumped into the floor beside the guy's boots were a potent incentive.

The man backed off, hands aloft to show he didn't want trouble.

'OK, OK, I get the message loud and clear,' he warbled nervously. 'But just remember what I said. The offer still stands until I leave town tomorrow morning.'

Daggert was still not interested. A meaningful click of the hammer urged the man to retreat. Once he had departed the drunkard slumped back into his seat. There was no denying the guy's offer was good: excellent if truth be told. And it had brought home an indisputable fact to the drinker.

Black Shadow was indeed a horse in a million.

The thoroughbred stallion was the only thing of any value he still owned. He owed his life to the animal. That was priceless.

But what the man had said struck a chord in Daggert's mind. A seed had been planted as to how he could avenge the brutal treatment dished out by that skunk De Vere. But he needed a clear head to work it out.

'A pot of hot strong coffee over here, barman, no milk but plenty of sugar,' he called out. 'And make it snappy.'

Jack Tranter heaved a sigh a relief. The expected conflagration somehow appeared to have dissolved. He didn't know why, nor did he care.

'I'll add some cookies to go with it,' replied the thankful bartender as he hurried about the task of brewing the strongest pot of Arbuckle's he could manage.

Over the next hour, with Daggert's brain quickly returning to normal, a scheme was shaped, a plan of action that would be foolproof if carried off properly.

And Black Shadow was the key.

Revitalized and raring to put his plan into action, Derby John set his trade-mark headgear at a spry angle. Suddenly he was a changed man. Gone was the surly grunting, the pugnacious attitude. In its place was a more amenable dude.

'Much obliged for your assistance, barman,' he warbled on leaving the saloon.

For once, Laughing Jack was stunned into silence. His gaping mouth flapped like a landed trout.

'Guess it was the coffee that done it,' Ike Barlow remarked. 'You'll have to re-member that for the next time we have a troublemaker park his ass in here.'

Outside, Daggert suddenly became aware how he looked and smelt when two sniffy dames stepped into the street to avoid him. But he was too animated to take offence. However, before that much-needed visit to the barber's shop, he needed to treat his horse to the equine grooming he had promised. The animal needed to be in top-notch condition for the forthcoming venture. His hand felt the leather poke of gold in his pocket. There was just enough left for them both to have a make-over, together with some supplies for the trek north back to Querida.

★　★　★

A circuitous route to the mining camp was essential to avoid the Crestone Desert. No way was he venturing into that cauldron again. Shadow had carried him out safely on the last occasion. But there was no point twisting the Devil's tail. Next time, Old Nick was likely to bite back.

So after leaving Alamosa he headed due east.

Fort Garland was also given a wide berth to avoid any human contact. Thereafter it was necessary to cross the Sangre de Cristo range by way of La Veta Pass. Swinging north, Derby John only made contact with other human beings on one occasion. The Herard ranch beside Medano Creek was the only settlement to challenge the hostile environment of the Crestone dunes on their eastern fringe.

The brief stopover came as a welcome relief for both man and horse. Daggert was able to enjoy his first home-cooked meal in a month of Sundays. Martha Herard sure knew her way around a kitchen. Abel, her husband, urged their visitor to stay overnight for some much-needed male chit-chat.

'We don't get many visitors,' bemoaned the ageing rancher. 'And I've gotten a new jug that's just aching to be uncorked.'

Daggert was eager to complete his journey and to achieve its sinister purpose. But Abel Herard's offer was hard to resist. One more night was not going to make any difference to the outcome. That skunk De Vere was still going to pay a heavy toll for his abuse. The fact that the victim had got what he deserved failed to penetrate the fixated villain's brain.

Following a rather heavy night, Daggert left the Herard ranch around mid-morning. Martha had packed some tasty vittles for the rest of the journey.

Unbeknown to the benevolent pair, they had also enhanced Daggert's billfold to the tune of thirty dollars. Less able to hold his liquor, Abel had fallen asleep in a chair, allowing his guest to make a search of the premises. He had found the greenbacks in a tin on the fireplace. The much-needed dough was impossible to resist and was quickly appropriated. It was no surprise that the thief was eager to leave next morning before the theft was discovered.

Querida hove into view a week after he had left Alamosa. Daggert had taken his time, to conserve the spirit and energy of his horse.

Evening shadows were threading a path across the valley of Grape Creek when he set up a temporary camp in a clump of ponderosa pine overlooking the mining settlement. From this vantage point, he could pick out familiar landmarks.

On the southern edge of town was Ma Kernick's lodging house where Daggert had taken a room. The assay office was on the far side of the town.

He did not want to make his play until after midnight when the town had settled down. If previous nights were to be relied upon, there should be a bright moon out by then. Once the first part of his plan had been accomplished, its silvery radiance would make his escape that much easier.

He opened a tin of beans, made himself comfortable and ate them cold with a spoon along with some hardtack biscuits. It was a frugal meal, but helped pass the time. Black Shadow, however, was given a supply of the finest grain, another solicitous gift from the gullible Herards. The horse needed to be in first-class form when the time came for him to show his mettle.

Once satisfied that quietness reigned over Querida, Daggert mounted up and circled round to the far side of the town. He tied off behind the wooden building of the assay office. A quick look around verified that nobody was about. Then he produced a thick iron bar to force open the back door.

This was the part that found his nerves on edge. No matter how carefully he prised and rived, there was no avoiding the crack and tear of rending woodwork.

Luckily, the premises were set back from the main street, away from other buildings. Daggert grinned to himself as the door lock disintegrated. He quickly slipped through the gap, dragging the door closed behind him. A hand delved into his pocket and produced a key. Yet another item that a search of his belongings had failed to unearth. Not the original, it was a copy.

The intruder knew the layout of the premises like the back of his hand. A door on the far side of this storeroom led into the main office where De Vere had installed a heavy iron safe. It was firmly bolted to the floor. No problem for an ex-employee with the means to open it.

Without the key his plan would have been impossible. Only dynamite would open a safe of that sturdiness.

An owl hooted somewhere in the distance. Outside in the street a dog barked. Just the normal sounds of a town at ease with itself. Nothing to bother an intruder.

Daggert cat-footed lightly across to the safe, knowing that it was his for the cracking. His features were taut with animated tension. The robber had chosen this particular Friday night because the safe was known to contain a substantial amount of money. The supposition was that Frisco De Vere had not altered his customary routine.

If that were the case, inside lay the monthly payroll for miners in his employ.

With bated breath the robber slotted the key into the lock. A brief pause, then he turned it. Following a solid click, the door swung open. A sigh of relief escaped from between puckered lips. Greedy eyes bulged.

But for all the wrong reasons. Where there ought to have been stacks of lovely greenbacks, only a handful of loose bills lay inside.

Desperately reaching forward he delved deeper into the safe. Bundles of official papers tied in pink ribbon abounded. But no hard cash. A snarl of anger hissed from between clenched teeth. That bastard De Vere must have altered the darned schedule. Daggert scooped out the notes which amounted to less than fifty bucks, and stuffed them into his pocket.

That was when the door to the assay room opened. A man stepped inside, a lantern held high above his head.

'What in thunder is going on here?'

snapped the startled newcomer. The gruff voice belonged to Israel Swann.

Daggert was similarly startled by the unwelcome intrusion. But he was the swifter of the two to gather his shaken wits. He grabbed the Remington and aimed the gun at the old-timer.

'Why are you skulking around here at this time of night, old man?' he rasped. 'A fella could get hisself shot.'

'Daggert!' came the startled exclamation. 'The boss has made me night guard.'

Daggert cursed. Yet another trick that Fate had played. Well, De Vere ought to have made a better choice than this old croker.

'More fool him for hiring a washed-out bag of bones like you,' mocked Daggert.

Swann wasted no more time in futile questioning. A gnarled hand fumbled with the whistle strung round his neck for just such a contingency as this. But the device intended to raise the alarm never reached his lips. A flash and a roar blasted apart the tight situation. Swann grunted. Staggering back he clung to the door-frame. A plume of blood erupted from his mouth as he slid to the floor.

'Serves you right, Judas,' snarled Daggert, gathering up the sack. 'Now I don't have to come looking for you.' His face cracked in a mirthless grimace. 'You had this coming for grassing on my affair with the lovely Letitia.' The hammer snapped back for a second time. 'And this one is for blabbing about my other little sideline.'

A second bullet finished the job.

But all that racket must have alerted somebody. Daggert wasted no time. He hurried outside and leapt on to the black horse that was patiently waiting.

Two men chose that very moment to emerge from their cabin on the far side of a vacant lot. Lodgepole Cooper and his partner Cactus Bob were prospectors who had been panning the creek outside the town for the last month. Just enough paydirt had been found to persuade them to stay on in Querida. The two men had been working late on the construction of a Long Tom that they intended trying out the following day. If successful, it would increase their yield of gold dust substantially.

'What's all the shooting about?' Cactus hollered, peering in the direction from where the gunfire had erupted. They saw a rider mounting up.

'Looks like some guy has robbed the assay office,' Lodgepole gasped out. The older prospector discarded the half-finished riffling box and hustled across the open ground towards the thief.

'D'yuh recognize him?' queried his young partner, pulling an old Navy Colt from his belt. Cactus Bob brandished the revolver in the general direction of the fleeing robber. Hauling back the hammer, he snapped off a quick shot. It was well wide of the mark. A cat screeched as the slug chewed a lump of wood from the tar barrel where it had been snoozing. The animal dashed off to seek safety away from the danger zone.

Caught off guard, the robber still managed to pump a couple of rounds at the approaching intruders. One lifted the kid's hat off his head, revealing a mop of greasy black hair.

The young prospector quickly hit the deck. He scrambled behind the barrel that the terrified feline occupant had so recently vacated.

The rising moon chose that moment to emerge from behind a cloud bank. Its silvery glow illuminated the robber's tense features. A vital aid to escape, the bright disc now proved to be a mixed blessing.

'He's got a look of that guy who used to work for De Vere in the office,' replied Cooper. Both men had sold their gold dust at the assay office, which meant they had come into contact with the guy. 'Thought I hadn't seen him around for a spell.'

Daggert snapped off another couple of shots before the less agile miner could join his partner. Without waiting to see the result, he urged Shadow to the gallop. The sooner he was out of here and on the trail the better.

A cry of pain informed him that this time his aim had been more accurate. A leer of satisfaction split his twisted features. But the heist had not gone as expected. Two bodies had been left behind, when the break-in ought to have been so simple. The real downer was that he had come away empty-handed. A rabid curse was whipped away by the night breeze.

But there was no point in crying over spilt milk. The most important issue now was to skip town and disappear into the sprawling wilderness of the San Isobel forestlands before the town marshal arrived on the scene.

Only the lightest of touches was needed to urge the horse into a full-blown gallop. Once clear of immediate danger he then settled down to a steady canter. In no time the gunman had faded into the gloom, leaving Cactus Bob to tend his injured confederate.

'You hurt bad, old buddy?' he enquired, bending over the fallen man. But there was no reply. A searching hand came away from the still form dripping with blood. A cry akin to that of a strangled chicken emerged from the kid's bearded face.

Lodgepole Cooper would not be joining his partner on any more gold strikes.

5

The Perfect Alibi!

The moon's radiant flush now made its presence felt.

Daggert cast a brief look at his watch. It told him that the time was a little after one o'clock in the morning. To ensure the perfect alibi he would need to be in Denver and supping with the eminent dignitaries of the town not later than late afternoon of that same day. It was asking a lot of Black Shadow. More than a lot, it was asking the impossible. But if he could achieve that, he would be home and dry.

Derby John was a gambler by instinct. He knew that he would be the chief suspect.

The killer's plan was to avenge himself upon De Vere by not only effecting a robbery but humiliating him in a court of law, face to face. In having the perfect alibi, at least he would be exonerated and could thumb his nose at the skunk. Free as a bird with no rap sheet hanging around his neck.

Now it was a question of survival. A robbery was one thing. But two killings? De Vere was an influential figure. He would have every lawman in the territory on his trail. The chances of avoiding arrest and the inevitable necktie party ad infinitum were slim.

These thoughts raced through Daggert's mind as he spurred off into the night.

From his experience of the previous trek south, the rider knew that the direct course through Cripple Creek, passing west of Pikes Peak, was the shortest route. It was also the most arduous. The way was tough and would be even tougher on his horse.

Shadow would not hesitate to negotiate the tortuous rocky trail but his pace would inevitably falter as height was gained. The downgrades were equally hazardous, with many hollows, loose stones and steep narrow ledges all liable to pitch a careless rider into the yawning gulfs.

Longer by about twenty miles but far easier was the route threading east to Pueblo. From there it was a straightforward push north along the Black Squirrel Wash and thence by way of Bracken Creek to Denver.

With this in mind, Daggert nudged his horse to a steady canter. Rippling black muscles were soon eating up the miles in a rhythmic pattern. The rider kept up a regular dialogue with his equine companion. From his racing days in Kentucky, Derby John understood that gentle words of encouragement would stimulate the animal in its historic quest for immortality.

As far as he was aware, no previous attempt had been made to establish an alibi in this manner. The ride from Querida to Denver would do just that and effectively put him in the clear.

Stopping only briefly for calls of

nature and to rest the black stallion, he headed up what had become known as the Goodnight-Loving cattle trail. He passed wide of three herds pushing north into Wyoming.

The drives were moving at a leisurely pace of no more than twelve miles a day. Daggert was aiming for that distance in a single hour.

The temptation to stop for a mug of hot strong coffee and a plate of son-of-a-gun stew was overwhelming. But he resisted, knowing that such delay would likely impede his task of establishing a foolproof alibi. Time was of the essence.

The final section through Castlewood Canyon was the most arduous because Shadow was noticeably flagging. His pace had slowed. Ever more frequently, gentle words of support were needed to keep the animal going. Daggert struggled to keep the impatience out of his voice.

Shadow's flanks were steaming, his shiny black coat swathed in a sticky layer of white lather. His nostrils were blowing hard, yet still the horse some-how kept going. Previously untapped reserves of energy were conjured up from deep within the stallion's psyche.

Daggert felt a genuinely sincere attachment to the horse, which enabled him to resist the impulse to use his spurs. He might be judged a robber and a killer, a scurrilous blackguard. But he still preferred the company of this loyal animal to any number of two-legged confederates.

Sensing that the remarkable journey was approaching its climax, Shadow seemed to find new strength. Nostrils flared as he picked up the pace. Over the next rise the town of Denver suddenly came into view. A huge sigh of relief issued from between the rider's clenched teeth.

Daggert took a quick look at his watch. It was approaching four o'clock in the afternoon. He drew the sweating horse to a halt and slid from the saddle.

By now De Vere would have informed the marshal and ordered him to dispatch telegrams to his counterparts in other places linked to the new communications network. By 1878, all major towns were connected to the telegraph system. Querida, unfortunately, was too small and remote. The nearest telegraph office was in Salida which involved a two-day ride. But that didn't help Daggert. His alibi needed to be established today, and the sooner the better.

His whole body ached. He fell to the ground, tight muscles contracting with the cramps. A cry of anguish was stifled as he vigorously massaged the offending limbs. But there was no time for any delay.

Delving into his saddle-bags, he extracted a new clean white shirt and brown corduroy trousers. They had been specially purchased for the next phase of his plan. A black necktie completed the transformation. The old shirt was used to clean up Shadow. A lathered mount would be noticed and arouse suspicion later. A quick wipe of his own dirt-smeared face and he was ready to venture into the town.

Remounting the trembling stallion, he walked the tired animal down the shallow grade and along the main thoroughfare of the mining settlement. The place was buzzing with feverish activity but nobody took any heed of the newcomer. The majority out on the street displayed the unkempt appearance of miners. In contrast Derby John Daggert presented the image of a successful businessman. His keen eyes flicked about, absorbing the hustle and bustle of the booming township.

He stopped one old guy who was hobbling across the street assisted by a stick.

'Which one of these joints is the swankiest in town?' he asked.

The greybeard looked the newcomer over with a jaundiced eye, noting the snappy attire.

'You going to a shindig, mister?' came back the cynical rejoinder. All Hardrock Hallam ever managed was some rotgut in one of the numerous dives catering to lowlife prospectors down on their luck.

'Got me an invite to a special event being given by the mayor.' Daggert had already prepared his little speech running it over in his mind beforehand. Making his presence known to the town's leading official was the crux of his plan. 'A fella has to dress right for these things.'

'Must be important,' said Hallam, leaning on his stick. Then an avaricious gleam suffused his leathery face. 'They discovered a new strike?'

But Daggert was impatient to complete his task.

'Ain't got no time for jawing,' he snapped out. 'You gonna tell me or not?'

'Just follow your picky snout down the street,' huffed the aggrieved jigger pointing his stick in the general direction. 'Any meeting of the bigwigs will be at the Golden Palace. You can't miss it.' Without any further comment, Hallam lumbered off to the far side of the street dodging the numerous wagons and horses passing by.

'This guy have a name?' Daggert called after the miner.

'Just ask for Jasper Logan,' the old timer threw back over his shoulder, adding with a chuckle, 'Me and the boys call him Jasper the Grasper, him being the local banker as well.'

Daggert smiled. Now that was a piece of news worth knowing.

'One more thing, old-timer.'

Hardrock stumbled to halt in the middle of the street and turned round as wagons and horses trundled by on either side.

'You and your buddies have a drink on me.' Daggert tossed a silver dollar into the air. The miner caught it deftly with his free hand, bit down hard to ensure it was genuine, then slipped the coin into a pocket. His stick was raised in acknowledgement as he continued his perilous journey. The Lucky Strike saloon was beckoning.

Daggert nudged his horse along the

busy street, keeping a watchful eye open for the suggested establishment. Another hundred yards and he spotted it, over on the far side, slap bang in the middle of town. The old jigger was right. The garish building painted in bright red and gold stuck out like a calico queen's chest.

He steered Shadow over to the hitching post closest to a water trough and tied off. Delving into one of his saddle-bags he produced some nutritious hard tack biscuits which he fed to the sweating animal.

'I'll make sure you get a proper feed once I'm done in here,' he whispered into the horse's ear. A gentle pat of the animal's majestic head was accompanied by a nervous, 'Now wish me luck, Shadow. I'm gonna need it.'

Then he mounted the boardwalk as a snickered reply sounded at his back.

He made a brisk check of his appearance in the reflection cast in a window. Dirt-stained boots were hastily cleaned down the back of his new pants. Last but not least, the trademark derby was cocked at a jaunty angle. Pausing momentarily to draw in a deep breath and steady his nerves, he then stepped inside.

Eyes widened as the opulence of the place gripped his senses. Decked out like a palace, the interior was meant to impress. It more than adequately succeeded. A pair of dazzling crystal chandeliers hung from the ornately painted ceiling. Rich velvet drapes covered the walls. In between, exotic tapestries from a bygone age added to the rather surreal atmosphere. Even the humble floorboards had received a liberal coating of rich mahogany varnish.

Johnny Daggert felt somewhat under-dressed for such a sumptuous setting.

A waiter was passing with a tray loaded with glasses of bubbly white wine. He was dressed in gold-braided livery. Daggert stopped him with a high-handed gesture. Exuding a degree of confidence he did not feel, the newcomer noncha-lantly scooped one up and took a sip whilst enquiring,

'I'm from out of town. The mayor's expecting me. Can you point him out, buddy?'

The flunkey, who was clearly used to being thus accosted, sniffed imperiously down his beaky snout. Wordlessly he casually aimed a languid hand towards a group of well-dressed dudes clustered around the billiard table.

Daggert's face lit up. Billiards. Now that was more like it. Poker might not have been Johnny's game, but potting billiard balls certainly was. His confidence took a sudden upward surge.

Three men attired in smart suits were gathered around the table. They were all set for a fresh game. A duo to play while the third refereed. Daggert's intention was to be included. Bulging girths straining at their fancy vests testified to the success these dudes had clearly achieved. All were puffing on large cigars.

The trickster had luckily stumbled upon a regular meeting of the mayor and his leading associates on the town council.

He was quick to notice that all had diamond stick pins in their silk cravats. Beaver-skin top hats graced their heads. These were men of importance, just the sort he needed to impress so that an interloper like himself stuck in their memory.

An initial reticence discarded, Johnny squared his shoulders. Rather than being overawed by such grand surroundings, Johnny Daggert suddenly felt at home. He had become used to mixing with the high flyers back in Kentucky, where he had enjoyed an equal measure of success.

Handling such pompous dignitaries in a frontier berg like Denver would be simplicity itself. After taking another sip of the wine he casually ambled across to the group. One of the men was setting up the balls on the billiard table while another chalked his cue.

'Which of you gentlemen is Mayor Logan?' Johnny asked, conveying an air of buoyant assurance that came naturally to the trickster.

A stout red-faced man put his cue down and peered at the newcomer.

'I am Jasper Logan,' replied the mayor in a voice reserved for underlings. 'To whom am I speaking?'

'My name is John Daggert. Derby John to my friends.' He tipped his hat while holding out a hand. The mayor automatically took the hand. 'I have been in Denver a few days but this is the first time my busy schedule has allowed me the pleasure of meeting the town's leading citizen.'

Daggert hooked out his watch and flicked open the lid. 'Time is money,' he warbled, 'and I have plenty to invest in a booming township such as Denver.'

This information saw the pompous official paying more attention. Anyone with money to invest was worth cultivating by Jasper the Grasper.

Daggert scowled. 'Darn it,' he exclaimed. 'My watch has stopped. Could any of you gentlemen confirm the correct time? You know what they say . . . ' He looked around expectantly as the three men hung on the newcomer's mesmerising tone. He had them hooked. 'Lose an hour in the morning and you will be all day hunting for it.'

The expected guffaws followed as the appropriate time was called out by the three men in unison. Johnny then proceeded to hook them in. Words of charm flowed off his tongue like sparkling champagne.

'I see you are about to play my favourite game,' observed the schemer. 'Perhaps I might be permitted to join you?' The question was uttered as a request that would be difficult to refuse without seeming rude.

The mayor offered his cue. 'Why not break off, Johnny,' he suggested. Daggert was pleased to note that his first name had now made him one of the boys.

'To make it more interesting,' said Johnny casually, 'how about a little flutter. Nothing too high, say erm . . . fifty bucks apiece?'

It would be churlish to decline the

proposition. So the bets were made and the game began. Johnny made sure he was partnered with the mayor. He wanted the guy to win. And win he most certainly would, with Derby John in support.

And so it came about.

An hour later Johnny Daggert was bidding his farewell to the trio of business men, a hundred dollars the richer. Not a huge sum, but enough to buy him a good meal and a bed for the night. Not forgetting a deluxe stall and the best treatment for Black Shadow. He had also secured the backing of the mayor in any venture that he might propose at some later date.

Most important, however, was that Derby John — robber, lothario, killer and confidence trickster — had established his presence in Denver at a certain hour and on a certain day, thus creating the perfect alibi.

Two days passed before Daggert felt the firm hand of the law on his shoulder. Sheriff Clint Ryker had received an urgent wire to look out for a man calling himself Derby John Daggert. The said personage was wanted for robbery and a double killing during its perpetration. A detailed description followed. The cable was signed by the town marshal of Salida on behalf of Frisco De Vere.

The assay agent and mine owner was well-known throughout Colorado on account of his successful enterprises.

The cable also went on to say that whichever town secured the villain's arrest, De Vere would travel there at his own expense to ensure a conviction. He was also offering to pay the arresting officer a substantial reward.

The name of Johnny Daggert had also become well-known in Denver over a surprisingly short space of time. This was due in no small measure to the man himself. And it was all part of his cunning plan.

When the lawman entered the hotel restaurant Daggert was enjoying a working breakfast with Mayor Logan.

Ryker headed straight for their table. All eyes followed this unexpected interruption to the morning repast.

Daggert had been wondering how long it would take the forces of law and order to suss him out. He was not worried in the slightest. It was all part of his plan to escape retribution. The only fly in the soup so far was his failure to secure any worthwhile profit from the venture. The robbery in Querida had been an abject failure. Hopefully, when everything had gone his way, that omission would be rectified with the gullible Jasper the Grasper's financial assistance.

Ryker stopped by their table.

'Something we can do for you, Clint?' enquired the mystified bank manager. It was clear that the mayor was on good terms with the lawman. 'Mr Daggert and I are engaged in some private business.'

The sheriff removed his hat. 'Sorry to interrupt, Mr Mayor,' he apologized. Logan had been instrumental in getting him elected. 'But I just received a cable from Salida about a serious crime that was committed down that way recently.'

'And what has that to do with us?' asked the official, whose tone had become somewhat frosty.

'The name of John Daggert was mentioned and his description tallies with this man.' Ryker's hard gaze fastened on to the other diner. A .45 Colt Peacemaker had leapt into his right hand. 'I'm arresting you, Mister, on suspicion of having committed robbery and a double murder. Are you coming quietly?'

'There must be some mistake, Sheriff,' blustered Logan. 'This man is a reputable businessman. Anyone can see that.'

'It's all right, Mr Mayor,' Daggert assured his associate. 'This sort of thing has happened before. A rival of mine who can't accept that a better man pipped him at the post has been trying to sour my good name ever since. This must be his latest attempt to get revenge. Don't worry. It will all be sorted out. You'll see.'

'That's as may be,' answered the lawman. 'But I have my duty. You are under arrest until such time as this claim of your'n can be proved in a court of law.'

'And when will that be?' asked Daggert.

'We have a resident judge in Denver based at the courthouse. Soon as the witnesses arrive the proceedings can begin.' Ryker wagged his six-gun, indicating that the accused man should accompany him. 'Until that time, I will have to hold you in the jailhouse. Your hogleg if you please,' the lawman added, holding out his hand.

Daggert filled it.

Logan was nonplussed by the suddenness of these startling events. Nonetheless, Johnny Daggert had made his presence felt and the mayor felt obliged to back his new associate's claim of innocence.

'I will ensure that you are well provided for in the hoosegow,' he promised the captive. 'Best food and reading matter to keep you occupied.'

'Much obliged for your support,' replied the grateful charlatan. 'You won't regret it. Everything will come out in court proving that I'm innocent as a new-born babe.'

The sheriff followed his prisoner out of the door. Daggert struggled to contain a smile. The situation was going just the way he intended. He forced a dejected scowl on to his handsome profile.

Curious eyes followed the pair down the street. In no time the true nature of the incident had rippled along the town's grapevine. This was a trial that was going to receive a lot of attention.

Daggert settled into his new rather spartan accommodation. He had expected no less and was prepared to accept the austere surroundings. But thanks to the generosity of his new business benefactor, for the next week he was able to pass a relatively comfortable sojourn.

6

The Trial

Frisco De Vere arrived in Denver the day before the trial started. Apart from dispatching innumerable cables to all points of the compass regarding the heinous crime in Querida, the only other message he had sent was to Joe Swann.

The scout was surprised to see Leif Erickson for the second time in a couple of months. After reading the telegraph cable, a liberal snort of his home-brewed moonshine was needed to get his head round the fact that old Israel was dead. Shot down by some thief when he had disturbed the critter. Leif stayed around to help his buddy cope with the harrowing news.

De Vere had arranged and paid for the funeral. The assay agent was sure that he knew the identity of the culprit and would keep Joe informed of developments. Apprehension of the killer was expected to be imminent in view of the blanket cables he had sent out.

Only a couple of days later, while Joe was at Fort Fetterman, did he receive the news that Derby John Daggert had been arrested in Denver. The trial was to be held on the following Tuesday if Joe could make it in time. The commander at the army base, Colonel Abel Mortimer, assured Joe that he could take all the time he needed.

So it was that on the morning of the trial in the Denver courthouse the young army scout came face to face with the man accused of killing his father.

The courtroom was packed to the rafters. Such cases always attracted a full house. It was standing room only at the back. Indeed, many potential spectators had been turned away. Enthralled faces peered in through the windows.

Joe recognized the accused instantly on account of his trademark hat. The guy was well dressed and sitting beside his lawyer. Jethro Cunningham was an equally spruce dude with pomaded hair and a waxed moustache. The two were having an earnest conversation, much of which appeared to be at the expense of the ageing, rather portly attorney sitting across the aisle with the two witnesses for the defence.

Daggert looked as if he hadn't a care in the world. Did his smarmy lawyer have an ace up his sleeve? Joe scowled at the guy's back, then took his seat.

De Vere sat next to the other witness. He had paid Cactus Bob's stagecoach fare and arranged for him to stay in a classy hotel. That was a first for the young prospector, who kept staring around the room, overawed by his part in the proceedings.

The noisy babble of voices was stilled by the court usher banging a gavel announcing in strident, commanding tones:

'Quiet in the court! All stand for Judge Angus Rowntree. The trial is now in session.'

A tall man with iron-grey hair strode

purposefully across the floor of the court-room, his boots echoing in the taut silence. The judge affected a lofty air of superiority as he took his position on a raised dais. Dark brown eyes peered over the rim of his pince nez spectacles, giving him the appearance of an ancient though wise old owl.

'Mr Fotheringay,' he bellowed.

The rotund attorney instantly jumped to his feet. 'Your honour,' he stammered out with a bow.

'You will please outline your case for the prosecution. And make sure that your account is brief and to the point. It is a bit early in the day to be falling asleep.' Roars of laughter broke out. The judge acknowledged the crowd's appreciation of his witticism with a wry smirk. His smile dissolved as his gavel slammed down to restore order.

'This is no place for hilarity,' he rapped out in a suitably grave voice. 'A man's life is at stake here. The next idiot who fails to heed the warning will be arrested for contempt.'

Total silence greeted this declaration. The crowd was well aware that Judge Rowntree was a man of his word. The judge then nodded for Mr Fotheringay to proceed.

So the trial got under way.

Joe avidly studied the reactions of the accused while accounts of the grim events unfolded. Daggert seemed surprisingly unmoved. He slouched in his chair as if it was nothing more than a drunk and disorderly charge that he was facing.

The first witness for the prosecution was Frisco De Vere.

He explained to the court how Israel Swann had discovered that the accused was stealing gold. When Daggert had been caught and punished, De Vere reckoned that that would be the end of the matter.

Being a cautious man, he had decided to change the wage delivery rota and appoint a night watchman. He explained that Daggert was in possession of confidential information that he might at a later date use to his advantage. Prompted by his attorney, the witness went on to make bold statements that were intended to throw an aura of guilt around the accused.

This was obviously a ploy for the purpose of leading the jury. Mention of his affair with De Vere's wife was deliberately avoided to save face.

The supposition reached was that John Daggert was clearly a bitter man who harboured a grudge. One way to expunge that simmering hatred was to rob his former employer. And so it had come to pass. It was assumed that somehow he must have obtained a copy of the key with which to open the safe.

The awful crime had led to the most heinous of results.

The witness stated further that he now greatly regretted putting an old man in charge of night security, even with enhanced remuneration. The court heaved a sigh of accord following this declaration. Glaring eyes fell upon the accused as De Vere resumed his seat.

Daggert's lawyer instantly jumped to his feet.

'I object, your honour,' Jethro Cunningham protested. His waxed moustache bristled with indignation. 'American law states that a man is innocent until proven guilty. My learned friend is assuming too much. Most of the evidence presented is circumstantial. Surely the guilt or otherwise of my client is for the jury to decide?'

'Objection sustained,' announced the judge. 'Counsel for the prosecution will restrict himself to the facts and not make assumptions on the basis of hearsay.'

'My apologies, your honour,' grovelled the obsequious lawyer. 'I will now call Mr . . . erm . . . Cactus Bob to the witness box.'

The prospector removed his battered hat and shuffled across the courtroom. The judge gave him a look of haughty disdain.

'Cactus Bob?' he blared out. 'What sort of a name is that?'

'A cactus has sharp spikes that will

86

give a man gyp if'n he don't take care,'
Bob declared with a flourish. 'Just like
me if'n any critter rubs me up the
wrong way.' He squared his youthful
shoulders.

Sniggers erupted around the court.

The judge sniffed impatiently. 'Give
your real name to the court, young
man.'

Bob coughed, his face turning a
brighter shade of beetroot. 'Do I have
to, your honour?' he burbled.

Judge Rowntree puffed out his
cheeks and responded to the query with
his most severe frown.

'Indeed you do,' came the angry
bellow. 'Now state it in full this instant
or I'll have you thrown in jail for
contempt of court.'

Bob hesitated for barely a second
before announcing in a low whisper,
'Horatio Wilkins Beauchamp.'

'Louder! We can't hear you,' snapped
the judge.

'*Horatio Wilkins Beauchamp!*'

For the second time the judge

smiled. 'Now I can see why you call yourself Cactus Bob.' Gales of laughter broke out in the court. Rowntree permitted the outburst for some moments before once again rapping for silence in court with his gavel.

'Proceed with your examination, Mr Fotheringay.'

The lawyer guided the witness through his testimony. He laid great stress on the fact that Bob had got a good look at the robber and could swear that he was indeed the accused.

Then it was Cunningham's turn to cross-examine the witness.

'Isn't it true Mr . . . Beauchamp . . . ' a sly smirk at the jury, 'that you have recently been forced to start wearing spectacles?'

The witness reluctantly nodded. 'But they's only for reading. I can see fine otherwise. It was him all right.' He was thinking of his dead buddy and that his killer was here in court.

'Is that so?' muttered the lawyer. He then pointed to a notice on the far side of the courtroom. 'What does that say?'

Without his spectacles, Bob was forced to screw up his eyes. 'No standing in court,' he said firmly.

Laughter broke out among the watching crowd. The lawyer purposely waited until the hullabaloo had died down before declaring bluntly, 'No sir! It says . . . Silence in Court.'

A shrug of the shoulders and another sardonic grimace for the jury's benefit effectively neutralized Bob's evidence. One further announcement was made to help sway the jury in Daggert's favour.

'And isn't it also true that it was dark when you observed the robbery, and from a distance, I might add?'

But the witness was not to be browbeaten into submission.

'The moon was out so it lit everything up,' Bob asserted, injecting a measure of grit into the avowal. He was sure in his own mind that Daggert was the killer. 'My dead buddy recognized him. And I am willing to swear on oath that he was the rat that killed poor old Lodgepole.' He shot out an accusing finger. It was aimed at the smirking face of John Daggert. 'I'll see you hang for what you done, yuh rotten bastard.' Cactus Bob appeared ready to leap off the stand and attack the defendant.

'The witness will control himself!' snapped the judge making good use of the gavel to emphasize his authority. 'Vigilante law has no place in this court.'

Bob's face reddened with embarrassment. 'S-sorry, your honour,' he stammered. 'Guess I got carried away.'

Judge Rowntree accepted the witness's apology with a curt nod.

Cunningham sighed. He had thought that the kid would buckle under his vigorous examination. But Cactus Bob appeared to have the hardy resilience of his namesake.

'No further questions, your honour,' he muttered resuming his seat.

The lawyer realized that playing his trump card would be the key to proving his client's innocence. If his assessment was correct, the jury were undecided. Under the present circumstances the verdict could go either way.

'Is that the case for the defence, Mr Cunningham?' enquired the judge, who was all set to make his summing up to the jury before they retired.

'I have one other witness to call,' the lawyer announced. The judge raised his bushy eyebrows in surprise. He peered around the courtroom.

'And where is this mysterious person, may I ask?'

'He wanted to remain outside until such time as he was called, your honour.'

'Go ahead then. But this is somewhat irregular.'

Cunningham whispered to the usher, who quickly left the room. Moments later, the door opened and in walked the mayor, Jasper Logan. An audible intake of breath could be heard rippling around the court as the town's leading official strode across to take his position on the witness stand.

Judge Rowntree was as stunned as the rest of the gathering.

The defence lawyer wanted to put on a dramatic performance to enhance the credibility of his witness's testimony. With slow deliberation he rose to his feet. Thumbs hooked into his suspenders, the lawyer then asked the witness to identify himself. Giving evidence in court in support of a man he had known for little more than a week made the mayor decidedly uneasy. It felt like he was on trial. All eyes were fastened on to him. Many present would love to see him brought down. He had no idea that this was all part of Johnny Daggert's plan.

'So, Mayor Logan,' the lawyer spoke in a stentorian voice, intended to convey absolute certainty that he was in charge here, 'will you tell the court when you first came into contact with my client?'

'It was last week,' Logan replied, casting an uncertain look at the accused.

'Can you be more precise?' said Cunningham. 'When exactly was this meeting?'

'I can certainly recall that,' replied Logan confidently. 'Mr Daggert's watch had stopped and he asked me and my associates for the time.'

The mayor paused in his delivery.

'So, Mayor Logan.' The lawyer smiled. 'Can you share it with us?'

After responding the witness went on to outline the nature of the meeting and the game of billiards that Daggert and he had easily won. All that was irrelevant to the lawyer. All he needed to establish was that his client was in Denver at a precise time on the very same day as the robbery took place in Querida.

'That will be all, thank you, Mayor Logan,' he said, cutting off the flow of the official's delivery. 'You have been more than helpful. I have no more questions for this witness, your honour.'

'What about you, Mr Fortheringay? Do you wish to question the witness?' asked the judge.

The prosecution lawyer was nonplussed. He had been outsmarted and knew it.

'None, your honour,' he muttered in a disconsolate voice.

'In that case I would also like to thank you, Mr Mayor,' declared the judge. 'I know that your time is valuable, so your presence here is very much appreciated.' He was well aware that it always paid for officers of the law to keep on good terms with the town council, who paid their salaries. 'You may go now, having ably assisted the law in its bounden duty to reach a just decision in this case.'

Logan acknowledged the compliment with a brisk nod as he left the room. The rather trying ordeal might have gone down without making him appear foolish, but he was glad to be out of there. From now on he would be much more wary of strangers who tried to curry favour.

'Could you now explain to the court, Mr Cunningham, your reason for calling the mayor to the stand?' requested the judge.

'With pleasure, your honour,' came

back the breezily confident reply. 'The robbery took place, according to Mr De Vere, at around one o'clock in the early hours a week ago last Friday.' Cunningham peered around at his audience, all of whom were hanging on his every word. 'On that very same day no less a dignitary than Mayor Logan has corroborated that my client was here in Denver, and that he had been here for some time.

'That being the case, I suggest to you, members of the jury, that it would have been a physical impossibility for him to have been in Querida — a mining camp that lies almost two hundred miles to the south of here.'

As the significance of this revelation struck home, an excited murmuring broke out in the courtroom. Some stern threats of rebuke were needed before the judge was finally able to restore order and Cunningham resumed his address to the jury.

'I therefore submit that John Daggert is innocent of all the charges brought against him and should be released forthwith. It is further proposed that this crime of robbery and murder was committed by person or persons unknown.'

Without further ado, counsel for the defence resumed his seat. Once again the courtroom erupted into ferment.

After the judge had given his summing-up the jury was instructed to retire and consider its verdict. The twelve good men and true were out for less than a half-hour.

'Have you, members of the jury, reached a verdict on which you are all agreed?' intoned Judge Rowntree in an appropriately solemn tone.

'We have, your honour,' announced the foreman, who was a local rancher. 'We find the defendant not guilty.'

Once again a throaty babble broke out in the courtroom. Struggling to make himself heard, the judge shouted above the hubbub that the prisoner was cleared of all charges and was free to leave the court without a stain on his character.

7

No Bucking the Law

Frisco De Vere could hardly believe his ears. He had been sure that Daggert would be found guilty. How in thunder had the bastard managed to reach Denver in such a short space of time? He racked his brain but failed to come up with a solution.

Cactus Bob was equally distraught at the unwelcome verdict. But what could they do? The law had spoken and that was that. He offered De Vere a doleful shrug of disappointment.

At that moment Daggert and his unctuous lawyer passed by.

'You feeling a mite down in the mouth, De Vere?' breezed the freed man, aiming a disdainful smirk at his old boss. He didn't wait for a reply. 'Some cases you win, some you lose. And this time you lost big time, sucker. Enjoy the ride home.' A sardonic chuckle accompanied the caustic remark.

De Vere just sat in his seat, dumbfounded. The not-guilty verdict had knocked all the stuffing out of him. All he could think to say was,

'How did you manage it?'

Daggert tapped his nose. 'Now that's between me and my best friend.' Then he moved on.

Joe Swann, who was sitting further back, was less accepting of the verdict. He was certain that Daggert was guilty. It was written all over the critter's leery features.

A growl of rage bubbled in his throat as he leapt to his feet. Pushing aside the lawyer, he lunged at the killer. Daggert was taken by surprise. A heavy blow struck him on the jaw. He staggered back crying out. Buckskin grabbed him by the scruff of the neck and hauled him up, his fist ready to deliver more of the same punishment to the oily face.

'Cease that immediately!' howled an

indignant voice from the back of the courtroom. 'There will be no brawling in my court.'

Judge Rowntree came striding down the centre aisle, his red face bursting with fury. His black cloak floated behind him, giving him the appearance of an avenging angel. 'Stop this instant, I say.'

But Joe was past caring. He ignored the order and landed another thudding blow on Daggert's face. Blood poured from a busted nose.

'Sheriff, arrest that man and throw him in the hoosegow,' the judge commanded. 'I will not have my court turned into a boxing booth. He can cool his heels in a cell for the next few days. Then the scoundrel will discover to his cost what happens to those who take the law into their own hands.'

Ryker grabbed the young hothead round the chest. A struggle ensued. But Joe managed to shrug him off. Once again he made to pounce on the odious object of his wrath. That was when the lights went out.

Joe Swann didn't wake up until some time later. His head felt like it had been kicked around by a loco mule. A lump the size of a duck egg had sprouted under his hat. He was splayed out on a grubby cot in the town jail. It was Deputy Merv Pfeiffer who had come to Daggert's rescue by laying his pistol barrel across the army scout's head.

The rattle of keys brought a look of pained anguish to the prisoner's ashen visage.

'Calmed down yet?' enquired Clint Ryker.

Joe groaned aloud while levering himself on to one elbow. He looked around.

'Where am I?' he mumbled, rubbing his head.

'You're in the jailhouse,' the sheriff replied handing the prisoner a mug of coffee. 'In this town we don't cotton to knuckleheads taking the law into their own hands. There ain't no room in Denver for vigilantes.'

The prisoner winced. But he still had

spirit enough to snap back, 'If'n that guy is innocent, my name ain't Buckskin Joe Swann.'

That piece of news brought a startled look to the lawman's leathery features.

'Swann, you say?'

Joe nodded, taking a welcome sip of the hot coffee.

'You a relative of the guy who was shot down in the Querida assay office?'

'He was my pa,' muttered the grief-stricken prisoner, wiping a tear from his bewhiskered face. 'He'd sent me a letter recently, expressing his suspicions about Daggert. He didn't trust the rat.'

'That don't make Daggert guilty,' countered the sheriff, who was a stickler for maintaining the letter of the law. 'And he was exonerated by a jury of twelve respectable citizens. You have to accept that.'

'I ain't accepting nothing,' retorted Joe, hurling the coffee mug against the wall. It shattered into a heap of tiny fragments. The brown liquid splashed across the brick wall of the cell.

On hearing the noise, Deputy Pfeiffer came running into the cell block, his pistol drawn. 'What in tarnation is all the racket?' he protested.

'Seems like our prisoner has no respect for law and order,' railed the sheriff.

'Then let him stay in here until such time as Judge Rowntree gets around to trying his case,' said Pfeiffer.

Clint Ryker's sympathy for the prisoner had evaporated like a desert mirage.

'That's exactly what's gonna happen. And don't expect no sympathy from the judge, mister. If'n there is one thing he detests, it's a skunk that thumbs his nose at the law.'

'You'll be lucky to escape with a fine,' added the snorting deputy. 'A month in the pokey is my guess.'

Joe lay back on his bunk, turning his head away.

When the two men returned to the outer office they had a visitor waiting to see them. It was Frisco De Vere. He was clutching an official-looking document in his hand. It boasted the official seal of the Colorado Law Society.

De Vere handed over the document, which Sheriff Ryker accepted. A look of blank puzzlement cloaked the lawman's grizzled features. He looked down at it, then at De Vere, seeking an explanation.

'I have been to see Judge Rowntree and persuaded him to grant me custody of your prisoner.' De Vere nodded to the release document. 'He was rather loath to concur with my proposal until I agreed to pay Swann's fine of one hundred dollars.' Delving into a pocket, he produced a wad of bank notes, which were also handed over.

The mine owner paused, allowing the import of his pronouncement to filter through into the lawman's turgid brain. It gave Ryker time to absorb these new and rather unsettling events.

'You've sure been busy, Mr De Vere,' he declared. 'The guy's only been in the slammer for two hours.'

'I feel responsible for his father's death,' explained De Vere, shuffling his feet. 'Old Israel was working for me, protecting my interests when the poor guy was shot down. I was certain Daggert had pulled the trigger. It came as a shock to discover he was here in Denver when the crime was committed. Like he said in court, there must be somebody else out there who also wants to get even with the critter.'

De Vere had clearly accepted the court's verdict, unlike Buckskin Joe. Nobody could have travelled that distance in such a short time.

'Glad to hear that somebody respects the law,' replied Ryker. 'You got plans for him?'

'You may think that I'm a generous dude, Sheriff,' De Vere puffed himself up, having regained his composure. 'But I ain't no soft touch. This fella is gonna work off his fine for me. That was a stipulation Judge Rowntree insisted upon. And if'n he refuses, the judge has promised to throw the book at him. And that means a Colorado chain gang for six months.'

Deputy Pfeiffer sucked in a deep breath. He shook his head, aiming his next remark at Ryker.

'Remember when I delivered Wild Jack Dupree up there last fall?'

The sheriff nodded. 'The warden gave me a personal tour of the site. I sure wouldn't want to be on the receiving end of that for a million bucks.'

De Vere smiled. 'I'll enjoy reminding him of what'll happen should he cause trouble.'

Joe Swann received the news of his impending release with mixed emotions. He was glad to be out of jail. But working off his fine for his benefactor by taking over his father's old position brought a lump to his throat.

How would he feel, treading in the grim shadow of death? Only time would tell. But he had been given little choice in the matter. Joe was only too well aware of the brutal realities of the infamous chain gangs.

There was still the problem of informing the colonel at Fort Fetterman. He had initially signed up for a year of duty with the army.

De Vere agreed to send a wire to the army post explaining the situation. So the deal to release the miscreant was concluded.

Around the same time Johnny Daggert had also come to a crucial decision. Denver was too hot a place for him at the moment.

On leaving the courthouse, his face resembled a portrait from Hell painted by the devil himself, the dominant colour being blood red. Bystanders gave him a wide berth. Their gaping faces exhibited a blend of suspicion and curiosity. A nearby horse-trough had removed most of the offending hue. But his mashed face still bore a blotched appearance akin to that of a slab of raw meat. Smoothing down his rumpled clothes, he headed straight for the bank.

Maybe the mayor was still eager to

do business? After all, he was an innocent man, wasn't he?

After enquiring if his new associate would receive him, a toffee-nosed clerk informed Daggert that Mayor Logan was unavailable for the rest of the day.

'So when can I see him?' rapped Daggert impatiently.

If the *gentleman* — the word was punched out with a sarcastic grunt — would like to make an appointment, the manager could spare him a few minutes on Friday morning. That was three days off. The lackey had obviously been briefed by his boss. Daggert immediately sensed that he was being given the cold shoulder.

Jasper the Grasper had quickly cottoned on to the fact that he had been set up to secure an alibi for the devious varmint. There was nothing he could do about that now. A verdict of not guilty had been given, which prevented the same charge being brought again without sufficient evidence to the contrary. But Logan was darned if the

107

guy was going to humiliate him more than he already had. The incident needed playing down so folks would not start asking awkward questions.

Daggert swung angrily on his heel and stamped out of the bank. He headed straight down to the livery stable at the edge of town. He was relieved to have paid up front for that de luxe revitalization promised for Black Shadow.

The rest of his dough had gone on the exorbitant fee demanded by that defence lawyer. At least the guy had come good. Unlike that chiseller of a mayor.

Daggert slammed his fist against the stable door. Stuff them all. The sooner he was out of this dump the better.

So Johnny Daggert headed north. He had heard about a new gold strike in the Black Hills of South Dakota up in Blacktail Gulch. Perhaps he would have more luck there.

After he had been released from custody in Denver Buckskin Joe and his new employer made their way south, back to Querida along with the subdued figure of Cactus Bob.

8

Express Rider

Two months after starting work for De Vere Holdings, Joe Swann had at last paid off his fine. It was a time for celebration. The Glory Hole saloon beckoned invitingly. Wandering down the street, Joe was greeted by a particularly dazzling female sashaying along in the opposite direction. She was no spring chicken, but none the less alluring for that. A hot-blooded guy, Joe could not ignore the fact that everything about the woman was in the right proportions.

'Mr Swann, isn't it?' purred the divine creature, tossing her mane of red hair back suggestively. 'This is the first time we have met.'

Joe could only return her greeting blankly. It was Cactus who provided him with some enlightenment.

'This is Mrs De Vere,' he said in a rather restrained voice.

'Please to make your acquaintance, ma'am,' replied the somewhat naïve young man. 'The reason we ain't met is because I've been working hard for your husband.'

'All work and no play . . . ' Letitia smiled, completely ignoring the more gawky Cactus Bob. 'I'm sure you know the rest. I'll have to tell Frisco not to be such a demanding taskmaster. We can't have a handsome fellow like you wearing himself out, now can we?'

The woman's eyes flickered beneath long dark lashes. Joe merely stood there, trying desperately to think of some witty reposte. Nothing came to mind.

'Perhaps we could meet up sometime and get to know each other more . . . intimately?' Her red lips pouted, mesmerizing the object of her attention.

Bob was well aware of the games that Madam De Vere played with those upon whom she sprinkled affection. He and Lodgepole had often talked about her indiscretions. The scarlet woman had never bothered unduly about keeping them a secret. Rumour had it that that was one of the reasons Derby John had suddenly disappeared before reappearing to wreak his revenge.

Buckskin had no inkling of her carnal leanings and just stood there, his fingers nervously twirling the fringes of his coat.

'Cat got your tongue then?' simpered the enticing female, wiggling her lithe frame.

The man was not given a chance to respond. At that moment two burly toughs came out of the saloon.

When Letitia saw who they were she immediately changed her manner, adopting a supercilious hauteur.

Her dainty nose poked the air.

'Mind your manners next time you jostle me, young man,' she said sniffily, pushing past Joe and his buddy.

'This jasper bothering you, Mrs De

Vere?' snarled the one called Snaggle-tooth Rayburn, flexing his muscle-bound arms. The other hardcase bunched his fists. The two men filled the sidewalk, a menacing presence and clearly eager for a set-to.

'Nothing I can't handle, thank you, boys,' she trilled rather nervously, hurrying on her way.

After the woman had vanished into the general store adjoining the saloon, Grizzly Jones issued a salutary warning.

'You boys keep away from that lady, you hear?'

'Mr De Vere don't take kindly to guys that trespass on to his territory,' smirked Rayburn. 'They end up somewhat regretting it.'

Grizzly laughed. It emerged as a mirthless croak. 'They sure do,' he concurred. 'That skunk Daggert got the message loud and clear.'

His sidekick was more circumspect. 'Pity the bastard escaped that murder rap, though.' At least Joe could agree with that notion.

Jones nodded. 'Nobody could have ridden from here to Denver in that short space of time.' The events of the trial had quickly spread and were now common knowledge in Querida. 'You jaspers heed my advice. You don't wanna get a taste of the boss's friend.'

'You sure don't,' echoed Snaggle-tooth.

Having delivered their unequivocal message, the two heavyweights then swung on their heels and strode off up the street.

'What in tarnation happened there?' exclaimed a bemused Buckskin Joe.

Cactus swallowed. 'Those guys are De Vere's bodyguards. They were the ones who gave Daggert a leathering after he was caught with his pants down. They make sure that everything and everybody toes the company line. You'd do well to keep away from that dame. She's bad trouble, like a hungry spider luring gullible flies into her web.'

Buckskin nodded. 'No chance of that. I've been walking out with Maggie

May Joplin. She's a waitress at the Leg of Mutton hash house.'

'I didn't know you were sweet on her.' Bob grinned, nudging his buddy in the ribs.

Joe blushed right down to the roots of his dark hair. 'I'm taking her to the Hoedown at Trelawney's barn next Saturday.'

Eager to get off the subject of his burgeoning courtship, Joe hurriedly entered the Glory Hole saloon. His smirking pal followed close behind. Both of them were now more than ready for that drink.

This was the first time since arriving in Querida that Joe Swann had visited a saloon. A spartan lifestyle had been assiduously pursued since the trial of Johnny Daggert. Owing money to anyone was anathema to Joe's way of thinking.

Old Israel had always taught his son to pay his way in life. *If'n you can't afford it, do without*, the old guy had advised. Now that he was free of his financial encumbrance, Joe felt that a huge burden had been lifted from his shoulders.

It was little wonder, therefore, that he had known nothing about the ensnaring charms of the lovely Letitia De Vere.

Over a few drinks the pair relaxed and forgot about their recent unpleasant experience. Joe also moved the conversation away from any teasing banter regarding his buddy's association with the adorable Maggie May.

But Johnny Daggert was never far from his thoughts.

Joe still hoped that some day, he would find his father's killer and go in pursuit of the rat. But Daggert had disappeared into the wild outback of the Western frontier. He could be anywhere by now.

Until such time as he learned of the killer's whereabouts, Joe was content to continue in employment with De Vere along with Cactus Bob.

The young prospector had lost the will to continue working his claim along

Grape Creek. Lodgepole Cooper had been the one who possessed shrewdness when it came to sniffing out paydirt. Now that his partner was dead Cactus had abandoned the claim, intending to move on.

De Vere felt he also had a responsibility towards the kid on account of the killing. So he had offered Cactus the now vacant job of night guard. The young man was more than happy to continue in the footsteps of Israel Swann. To ensure that he was well protected, Bob had been given a shotgun in addition to the whistle.

For the next few months Buckskin Joe continued working for De Vere.

Ore prospecting was not one of his areas of expertise. But he was a good horseman, and could handle firearms. Being an army scout, he was also a master when it came to navigating through difficult terrain. De Vere had needed somebody he could trust to communicate with the managers of his various enterprises.

Correspondence with the mines was slow in view of the remote situation of the workings. There was always something to impart regarding new ore discoveries, assaying certificates, problems encountered in the diggings and delivery of important documents, to name but a few things.

Delays in maintaining contact were frustrating to the go-ahead businessman.

Over a decade earlier the old pony express had been an essential cross-country service between St Joseph and Sacramento, carrying the US Mail. It was far quicker than the Butterfield stagecoaches. But the job was perilous and the riders were subject to attack by Indians. They had all been young men eager for adventure and were highly respected, bold champions of their generation.

Progress in an expanding United States, however, quickly overtook the scheme. By 1861 the telegraph lines stretching across the country had curtailed the heroic activities of the pony express after only eighteen months.

But such a service was still needed in far-flung outposts where no such modern technology as the telegraph could reach.

Joe Swann had admirably filled that vital role.

The army scout became a well-known figure in the numerous mining camps operating in the foothills of the Sangre de Cristos Mountains. More to the point, he could deliver everything on time.

Some of the independent prospectors panning the mountain streams began using Joe as a means of conveying their ore samples back to Querida. The express rider earned an additional fee for this service, and it enabled the prospectors to carry on with their search for paydirt without interruption.

De Vere was happy for his messenger to branch out in this line of work provided it did not impinge on his official duties.

Everyone, it seemed, was a winner.

But like all ideal schemes, there was

119

always a drawback.

Delivering documents and papers was one thing. Nobody was particularly interested in such items. But the carriage of potentially valuable ore samples was a different matter entirely.

One miner who had failed miserably in his quest for easy lucre was a half-breed Mexican-Apache by the name of Chico Sanchez. The brooding prospector was jealous of his more successful associates. So one day he decided to do something about it. The express rider regularly passed the end of Wild Horse Gulch where Sanchez had set up his camp.

Buckskin Joe's next run was around noon of the following day. Sanchez intended waiting for him with a loaded gun.

The next day the 'breed took up his position on a ledge overlooking the trail at the entrance to the gulch.

East of Querida the land rose steadily as the grassy foothills surrendered to a dark-green terrain where endless stands of ponderosa fine and Douglas fir prevailed. Even though spring was here it was still cold, so Joe pulled his sheepskin coat tightly around him.

Within the deep ravines, the sun struggled to make its presence felt. Care was needed where the trail narrowed and the ground noticeably steepened. A couple of disturbed chipmunks gave the passing rider dirty looks as they scooted out of his way. Overhead a chickadee swooped by for a quick peek at the intruder.

Here in the clefts and gravel beds of the chattering streams was where the paydirt settled and where many of the mines were located.

But Chico Sanchez was as inept at bushwhacking as he was at gold prospecting. He ought to have remembered that his sombrero had a high crown and should have been removed. Peering over the top of the boulder behind which he was hiding, both hat and gun were clearly visible from down the trail.

A professional scout like Buckskin Joe Swann took heed of everything. As a consequence his rifle was always at the ready, resting across his knees. He was always on the alert for irregularities in the landscape. It might be the sudden flight of birds out of a tree, sunlight reflected off a metal gun barrel or steam rising from lathered horses supposedly hidden from view.

In this case the sombrero poking above the rock was a dead giveaway. Somebody was up ahead, waiting to ambush him. Joe was carrying a sizeable number of ore samples at the time. Clearly the word had spread to the wrong ears.

The approaching rider waited until he was within range before bringing up the long gun and pumping a couple of shots at the obvious target. Any proficient thief would have used the hat as a decoy. Not so Chico Sanchez. The headgear flew into the air. The bush-whacker's rifle was lost, clattering down amongst the rocks. So stunned was the failed robber at having been caught out that he fell off the ledge right into the path of his intended victim.

Joe's horse ground to a halt in front of the woebegone ambusher. His gun covered the sorry excuse for a *bandido* as he ordered the critter to stand up.

'Guess you figured on getting your dirty hands on some easy loot, eh?' Joe rasped.

Sanchez gurgled and groaned. His dust-shrouded corpulent frame swayed alarmingly.

'You're going back to Querida with me. The boss can deal with a skunk like you.'

'No, no, please, *señor*,' wailed the wretched 'breed. 'Not that. I will do anything you say, be your slave, lick your boots. But please do not turn this poor failure over to Señor De Vere and his bodyguards.'

The vehemence of the guy's pleading surprised Joe. His round face had turned white with fear. Joe knew the boss was a strict disciplinarian, although he had discounted the brutal stories as those emanating from guilt-ridden offenders. That was until he had come across Snaggletooth Rayburn and his ugly sidekick, Grizzly Jones. This guy had certainly wanted to rob him and deserved to be punished. Yet now he felt sorry for the poor sap.

Perhaps it was the 'breed's total ineptitude. Joe had never previously encountered such a clumsy bandit. And the clown was scared stiff. Perhaps he had good reason to be terrified, mused Joe.

The express rider considered the dilemma now filtering through his brain for a short minute before coming to a decision.

'OK, *amigo*, I'm gonna let you go,' he rapped out. His raised hand curbed the jigger's elation. 'But I see your ugly mug around here again, I'll feed you to the buzzards.'

'Thank you, *señor*,' warbled the 'breed, bowing low and grasping Joe's hand in gratitude. 'I go pack up camp now. There is a new gold strike up north in the Black Hills. Perhaps Sanchez have better luck there. You not see me again, I promise.'

'I better not,' growled Joe, trying to keep a smile off his face. 'Now git!'

The fat man hustled away as fast as his short legs could waddle.

Joe waited until he was out of sight and not likely to change his mind. But his Winchester remained trained on the entrance to Wild Horse Gulch, where he stayed for the next five minutes. Satisfied that Sanchez had got the message, he then continued with his journey.

This was an event he would keep to himself. Mulling over the prospector's genuine fear, he saw that Frisco De Vere would also require careful handling. Everything the guy did was certainly within the letter of the law, but perhaps not within its moral intent. He could be generous with those who supported him, and equally ruthless with malingerers and troublemakers. Considering those heavyweight bodyguards at his back, Joe could now readily understand Sanchez's fear.

The trek around the various mining

projects was completed in three days. Once done, Joe wasted no time in getting back to Querida. He was anxious to see Maggie May. The sun was setting over the backdrop of serrated mountain tops as he rode into the mining settlement.

De Vere was in the assay office when he got back to town.

'Any problems?' he enquired, without looking up from the ledgers he was studying. A glass of whiskey by his elbow complemented the cigar burning away in an ashtray.

'Charlie Vickers up at the Turret mine has had a rock fall, but he reckons it will be cleared by tomorrow.' Joe dumped a pile of letters and ore samples on the counter. 'And Powder Jack Garfield has discovered a new seam branching off the main shaft in Rockwood Canyon.'

De Vere nodded. 'A good man, Garfield,' he muttered, looking up from his work. 'Anything else?' He poured out another glass of whiskey and pushed it across to the messenger. De Vere was an astute businessman and knew how to treat good employees. And Joe Swann, like his father before him, was one of the best.

Joe smacked his lips, acknowledging the top quality of liquor he was drinking. He purposely did not reveal the set-to at Wild Horse Gulch and the fact that he had shown mercy to the perpetrator. That was not De Vere's way, as Sanchez had so eloquently displayed. The incident would remain a secret, unless Sanchez reneged on the deal.

He delved into the heavy saddle-bags and pulled out the ore samples collected during his rounds. Only one other item needed checking further.

'When I delivered this letter to an independent prospector working a claim up in Dead Man's Draw, the guy refused to accept it. Said he wasn't prepared to pay the mailing fee. He knew who it was from and had no intention of lending money to his no-account brother.'

9

Hand of Fate

De Vere took hold of the missive and idly read the name of the addressee. He knew about Aaron Baker and was party to the bizarre circumstances that had brought him to Colorado. He went on to explain the facts as he knew them.

'Baker reckoned that he and his brother had split and gone their separate ways after the guy had stolen money off their folks.' He paused, turning the letter over. 'There was a fight over his younger brother's gambling debts and Aaron was shot in the arm. When their father tried to grab the gun it went off, killing the old man. It was an accident, but Aaron always blamed his brother and never forgave him.'

De Vere went on to explain that

Aaron Baker had received letters before, all asking for money. He had reluctantly complied. Being asked to shell out the high charge that his no-good brother had landed him with was clearly the last straw.

Where US Mail deliveries were involved, it was normal for the sender to pay the mailing fee for letters. An extra charge was imposed that was the recipient's responsibility should the sender post the letter without purchasing a stamp. That fee grew even larger when private mail deliveries became involved, as was the case here.

All of a sudden, De Vere suddenly cut short his story. The blood drained from his face. Joe didn't notice the boss's sudden change of manner. He was too busy sorting the other papers into their respective pigeon holes ready for filing.

'This writing . . . ' De Vere's voice crackled with shock. His eyes widened as he stared hard at the inky scrawl. Joe instantly picked up on the tremulous inflection. He looked up. The boss poked a shaking finger at the address on the envelope.

'I recognize it.'

A thoughtful frown spread across Joe's face as he waited for the boss to continue.

De Vere refilled his glass, gulping down the hefty slug of whiskey before replying,

'The letter was written by John Daggert.'

Without thinking, Joe grabbed it and studied the writing. It meant nothing to him as he had never worked with the guy. But De Vere certainly had.

'You sure about this?'

'Never more so,' De Vere snapped. 'I'd recognize that handwriting any- where.'

A question then leapt into Joe's mind. Why was it addressed to Aaron Baker?

De Vere read his thoughts.

'Daggert must have changed his name after he disappeared from the family home.' Joe had to agree. It seemed like the only logical explanation. 'That was how he landed up in Louisville, Kentucky and took on a whole different lifestyle. Aaron must have come to Colorado in search of his wayward brother.'

'You better open it, boss.' Joe's voice sounded distant, disembodied, as if it belonged to somebody else. Gingerly he handed the letter back. 'Maybe it will give us a clue as to where the rat is hanging out.'

De Vere opened the envelope with great care as if something might suddenly jump out and bite him. Inside was a single sheet of paper which he likewise tentatively extracted. After reading the brisk message, he handed it to Joe for his assessment.

It read:

Dear Brother,

I am writing to ask you to send two hundred dollars. I have been thrown in jail. Its only for being drunk and disorderly, but I ain't got any dough for the fine. This place is under vigilante law and the guy in charge says if I don't pay up within a month he's gonna put me to work on a chain gang in one of his mines until I've worked off the fine. I know we ain't seen eye to eye for some time. But I'm still your only kin. So I'm begging you to help me out.

Best regards from your affectionate brother,
Abraham

Joe sucked in a deep breath. Perhaps if Aaron Baker had read the letter he would have submitted. Joe realized that it was his good fortune that such a situation had not occurred. Had the guy paid up, he would never have discovered the whereabouts of his father's killer.

So Derby John Daggert was really called Abraham Baker.

It took some moments for the momentous revelation to sink in. When it did hit home, the truth was that the killings in Querida weren't Daggert's — or Baker's — initiation into terminal gunplay. Not that any of that mattered now. The main thing was that finally, after six months, Joe had discovered where the pesky varmint was hiding out.

A harsh guffaw issued from between his clenched jaws. The killer wasn't exactly in hiding. It had turned out to be a stroke of luck that he was stuck in a vigilante jail. Not if Buckskin Joe Swann had any say in the matter. The skunk had escaped the hangman once, but he wouldn't escape justice again.

But this time, he would not have some smart-assed lawyer to get him off the hook. Termination would be administered in the form a bullet from Joe Swann's six-shooter.

His hand strayed to the gun on his hip. Without thinking, he drew the revolver and flicked back the loading gate, spinning the chamber. A deft twirl on the middle finger and the gun was returned to its holster.

But first he would have to get the guy out of jail. A brief glance at the envelope revealed that it had been mailed from Deadwood, up in the Dakota Black Hills.

'You got plans, Joe?' enquired an impressed Frisco De Vere, sensing the other man's purpose.

'Reckon I have, boss, if'n it's all right with you.'

There was no hesitation from De Vere. He knew exactly what those plans entailed. He reached a hand into his jacket pocket and removed the billfold. He extracted a bunch of notes and handed them over.

'Here are your wages that are owing, plus a bonus for the good work you've done.'

'Much obliged, boss. I don't like leaving you so quickly, but there's a bullet here,' Joe tapped the holster, 'with this rat's name on it.'

De Vere nodded, then drew out some more dough. The mine owner knew in his heart that Daggert had somehow contrived to escape justice. He just didn't know how he had managed it.

'Give him one for me. Your pa was a solid and loyal man. He didn't deserve that. Here is another two hundred bucks to pay his fine. It'll be cheap at the price to see that skunk get his just deserts.'

'Mind if'n I take Cactus Bob with me?' Joe asked, pocketing the money. 'I could use some back-up and the kid's no slouch with a hogleg. Me and him have been practising at the firing range behind Jubal Kade's gun shop.'

'He lives up to that nickname, eh?' smirked De Vere.

'Guess he does at that,' agreed Joe.

'If'n he's agreeable then so am I. Just make sure this caper don't turn into no wild-goose chase.' He waved Joe off the premises. 'And good hunting.'

When Joe made his proposal to the new assayer, Cactus Bob couldn't wait to hit the trail. The thought of catching up with old Lodgepole's killer was stimulus enough to see him hurrying over to the cabin they had shared to collect his gear. But he still had one word of caution for his new buddy.

'Have you told Maggie May about this?'

Joe's mouth hit the floor.

'Gold-darn it!' he exclaimed. 'In all the excitement, I clean forgot.'

'Best get to it, buddy,' advised Bob with a sympathetic regard. 'She ain't gonna be too pleased about you skipping the Saturday dance.'

Joe hurried across the street to the diner where Maggie was a waitress. He gestured through the window, trying to catch her attention. The girl could see that her new beau was agitated about something. Making an excuse, she indicated for him to meet her round the back.

'What's the matter, Joe?' the concerned girl asked. 'You sure are stirred up about something.'

Joe sucked in a deep breath. His emotions were all in a tangle. On the one hand he wanted to hunt down Johnny Daggert for however long it took. But he was smitten with this delectable angel and was loath to disappoint her.

'Fact is . . . ' He hesitated. Hat in hand, he shuffled his feet nervously. 'Fact is I have to go away for a spell.'

'How long for?' came the blunt demand.

'Could be a few weeks, or a few months. It all depends.'

'Depends on what?' Maggie was becoming rather exasperated.

'On whether Cactus Bob and me run down the critter that shot my pa. We've found out that he's in Deadwood — '

'But that's way up north, in the Dakotas!' snapped the girl.

Joe shrugged. 'I hate to leave you at such short notice,' he apologized, 'but I ain't got no choice. If'n I stick around here, he could disappear.'

Maggie suddenly relented. She knew that acting all indignant was selfish. A lovely half-smile lit up her silken features.

'What am I thinking? Of course you have to go. I'm glad you told me. Don't worry, there'll be other dances. And I'll still be here when you come back.'

Joe kissed her lightly on the cheek. It was the first time they had experienced any sort of intimacy together since walking out. Before he could turn away she caught his head in her hands and planted a real kiss on his lips. Joe felt as though his feet left the ground as a mesmeric tingle coursed through his whole body. When he came back down to earth an hour later, in effect a few seconds, her bewitching smile urged him to get started.

He was walking on air as he wandered back to join his partner at the livery stable.

10

Twice Beholden

Johnny Daggert finally reached the Black Hills almost six months after his rather dubious exit from Denver. He was still unsure whether the trial had been a success or a failure. The whole episode somehow appeared unreal. Yet there was no disputing it had happened.

Sure, he had put one over on Frisco De Vere. His spectacular ride on Black Shadow had turned him into an overnight sensation, although no mention of this was made in the newspaper reports that followed the trial. Much as he would have enjoyed trumpeting the horse's remarkable stamina, that had to remain his secret. He could always use the same stunt again in the future.

Having literally got away with murder, the robbery and its unfortunate aftermath were now safely tucked away in the unsolved crimes file.

On the other hand, he had come out of it feeling ill at ease. All his dough was gone. His mangled visage had the appearance of a rare steak for weeks afterwards, and folks had treated him like a pariah. Derby John reckoned that he ought to have been fêted like a big shot and compensated accordingly for his mistreatment by the law. He had received nothing, not even a miserable nickel for all those newspaper articles.

That's right. He felt hard done by. Johnny Daggert had come to believe in his own duplicity. He had forgotten that in effect, he was guilty as sin and ought to have received a neck-stretching.

For the next few months he had survived by becoming a lone-wolf road agent. Only solitary travellers were waylaid and their goods and chattels appropriated. He was quite proud that he had become pretty adept at pursuing a career outside the law. There was even a Wanted dodger out for his arrest.

Only once had the outlaw been forced to shoot a man.

He shrugged on thinking back to the incident. It had been the guy's own fault. He shouldn't have resisted. Although when Johnny discovered a leather pouch containing gold worth over 1,000 bucks in the dead man's saddle-bag he could readily understand the poor sap's reluctance to surrender without a fight.

Now, at last, he was in the Black Hills country.

Daggert and his buddy soon found themselves entering the steep-sided valley of Blacktail Gulch. For as far as the eye could see, where recently the slopes had been cloaked with dense pine forests, only bare stumps now remained. Numerous camps had sprung up along the whole length of the meandering valley. All the trees had been cut down to produce pit props and building material.

The principal town was Deadwood, a drab sprawl of half-finished shacks, none of which had received a lick of paint to relieve the gray bleakness. This place had been built purely to serve a transient population whose sole aim was to grab what the land had to offer before moving on to the next gold strike.

No flowers had been planted anywhere to relieve the drab monotony of the place. Heaps of gravel were piled high everywhere, hewn from the earth by the sweated labour of hard-rock miners. Nobody cared about the despoliation of the landscape so long as it released paydirt in sufficient quantities. Log flumes snaked down from the heights above, where water to wash out the gravel had its source.

Few people stopped their toil to study the newcomers who received scowls from those who did bother to look up from their endless hard graft. Just two more unwelcome miners to swell the masses already here. Once through the chaotic ravages inflicted on the landscape, they paused momentarily to survey the mining settlement.

It was late summer now, and the

leaves were already starting to fall. Deadwood was teeming with prospectors who thronged the narrow main street. Daggert and his new partner threaded their way between men dragging mules piled high with mining gear. They could almost smell the gold dust in the air.

Sure there was plenty of wealth in the Black Hills. But it took a heap of backbreaking toil to extract paydirt from the hard ground. The shabby, down-at-heel appearance of those leading the animals testified to the tough life they led.

That was not Derby John's idea of how to get rich.

He couldn't help noticing the large array of saloons, all there to relieve the miners of their hard-earned lucre. Johnny was a gambler by nature. It was in his blood. And his pockets were all but empty. His bulging eyes glittered with avarice. He had clearly not learned the harsh lesson of his previous experience at the gaming tables, which had resulted in ignominy.

Johnny's partner noticed the gleam in his sidekick's gaze.

'You feeling lucky with the cards, *amigo*?' Chico Sanchez enquired in that lyrical high-pitched accent.

'I sure am, buddy,' Johnny breezed, tapping his lucky hat. 'You'll see. Derby John Daggert will be rolling in green-backs faster than you can skin a rabbit.'

The two men had met by chance a few weeks previously.

Daggert's horse had been negotiating a tricky ledge through Buffalo Gap in the Osage Mountains. A surprised buzzard had spooked the animal. Shadow had reared up on his hind legs, unseating his rider, who had tumbled into a deep narrow ravine. Daggert was concussed, with a dislocated shoulder. He had regained consciousness knowing that his situation was dire in the extreme. He could not move. And unless some other traveller came though the gap soon, he was finished.

That someone had been Chico Sanchez, who was also bound for

Deadwood. Daggert had given up hope of being rescued when the half-breed noticed Black Shadow standing on the edge of the ravine. His owner must have fallen into the ravine. Sanchez called down into the gloomy depths. A muted groan floated up from below.

There was no way that the stout Mexican could get down there. But he had a rope and a strong mustang. After securing the rope around the saddle horn Sanchez lowered it into the dark chasm. With his good arm Daggert managed to circle the loop around his body. The tough quarter horse then pulled him out of what he had feared would be his grave.

After much hum-ing and hawing, Sanchez had managed to reset the dislocated bone. But the whole dire episode had taken a lot out of Daggert. So they had rested up in Buffalo Gap for a couple of days until he was recovered sufficiently to continue. During that time, the portly Mexican had proved himself to be an able cook.

Heading in the same direction, the unlikely duo had decided to team up.

Sanchez shrugged at his partner's blasé comment regarding his prowess as a saloon card-wielder. He was not a gambler himself but had no reason to doubt his new *compadre*'s skill with the pasteboards.

'You coming to watch an expert at work?' Daggert asked his buddy.

Sanchez shook his head. His own gaze was focused on a Chinese eatery called Lee Fong's Chop House. His belly rumbled at the thought of all that lovely grub. He had been introduced to Chinese food while working with the coolies on the Central Pacific Railroad in California.

The two parted company, arranging to meet up outside the Lucky Strike saloon.

* * *

It was a couple of hours later and Chico had just left the Chinese diner. He rubbed his belly. That sure was one of the best meals he had eaten. He was about to cross the street to see how his partner was faring in the saloon when a fracas broke out. Three burly jaspers were dragging a fourth man out of the saloon. He was barely conscious with blood dribbling from a cut on his head.

It was Johnny Daggert.

Sanchez gasped with shock. He drew back into the shadows and watched as the three toughs bundled his partner down the street. Plenty of others were also watching the event. Sanchez joined them to follow the small procession from a distance. After seeing Johnny being flung into the lock-up, his devious brain was working out how to extricate his new partner from his predicament.

After recovering from the alarming jolt, Sanchez made some tentative enquiries to determine what had occurred. News travelled fast in a place like Deadwood.

It emerged that, as in previous forays

at the poker tables, Daggert had become frustrated when his stake had dwindled. After accusing the house gambler of cheating, he had upset the table and all its contents. A fight had ensued. Before any permanent damage could be done to either party, Daggert had been slugged over the head by one of Judge Pikestaff's bully boys. The judge was the law in Deadwood, which was run by a bunch of hard-nosed vigilantes.

A trial had been convened on the spot, with Pikestaff presiding. Most important was that a fine of 200 bucks had been imposed. If the prisoner failed to pay up within a month he would be put to work on a chain gang in one of the judge's mines.

Sanchez shivered at the thought. Stuck underground, chained up at a vigilante court's behest was no laughing matter. But what could he do? Two hundred! He was no gambler, and couldn't hope to earn that much *dinero* in the time available.

Ten days passed. Chico Sanchez still hadn't figured out how to help his partner. Then it struck him. If'n he couldn't obtain the dough by legitimate means, there was always the other way. It took a few jolts of his favourite tequila to summon up the nerve to do the only thing he could think of to obtain the money.

That same day he rode out of town up Spearfish Creek until he reached a lonely stretch of the trail. He chose a spot where it narrowed to single file. There he settled down behind some boulders to await the arrival of a lone prospector bound for Deadwood with his hard-earned poke.

Various riders passed his place of concealment, but all were in twos and threes. The only single rider was young and looked like a tough hardcase. Not the sort to surrender his stash willingly.

The bushwhacker had almost given up when an old jigger perched atop an ancient burro ambled into view. Well past the age of spirited resistance, he made an ideal victim. Sanchez was loath to rob the old guy, but his partner's need was the greater.

As the trundling rider drew closer, Sanchez tied a bandanna around his mouth. Then he remembered just in time to remove his large sombrero as the last foray into lawbreaking flashed through his mind. Girding himself up with a deep breath, the bushwhacker leapt out in front of his target brandishing a pistol.

'Hold up there, *hombre!*' Sanchez declared in his gruffest voice. 'Raise your hands and give me your poke. Any funny business and it will be the worse for you.' He waved the cap-and-ball Navy Colt menacingly.

The prospector grunted. 'How can I hand over the goods with my hands stuck up here?' he questioned. It was a logical enquiry.

Sanchez frowned. Tentatively, he circled the ragged jasper on his equally wretched mount, noting the bag tied to the saddle horn.

'That look mighty like bag of gold to me,' he said, eyebrows raised.

The prospector shrugged. 'Best take a look then, hadn't you?' he grumbled. 'It took me the better part of this summer to dig out.'

Sanchez waved the gun menacingly, then grabbed the bag and stepped back. Shaking fingers gingerly pulled back the drawstring, allowing Sanchez's greedy peepers to fasten instinctively on to the glittering contents of the bag. A gasp issued from his gaping mouth. Gold has that effect on all who have tried their luck with a filtering pan. The distraction of the robber was enough to encourage the old jigger to draw his own pistol: a heavy Colt Dragoon that had seen better days. The gun rose, the hammer snapped back.

That sound was enough to warn Sanchez of the danger he was in. His own pistol, which was cocked and ready, spat flame. The single hunk of lead was sufficient to punch the feeble old prospector off his burro. His body slammed into the ground.

Sanchez just stood there. He was shaking with nervous tension. This was the first man he had ever killed. Desperately he gulped air into heaving lungs. Then he emptied out the contents of his sizeable stomach.

'Crazy old fool,' he ranted at the still corpse. 'Why you make Sanchez do that?'

But the awful deed had been done. Quickly Sanchez looked around to ensure he was still alone. Satisfied that the heinous crime had gone unnoticed, he dragged the bag of bones into the rocks, where it would be hidden away from prying eyes. He removed the saddle from the burro and slapped the animal hard on the rump. The startled beast skittered off back the way it had come. Anybody finding it would assume it had wandered away from its camp.

Once he had regained his composure, the bushwhacker knew that he had to act quickly. There was still time to reach the assay office and have the gold assessed and changed into greenbacks.

He mounted up and returned to Deadwood at the gallop. Speed was of the essence in case the old dude's body was discovered and a hue and cry raised. Sanchez had to force himself down to a steady walk along the main street to avoid unwelcome attention. All the same, he still imagined that accusing eyes were fixed on him. But nobody gave the solitary rider a second glance.

The transaction at the assay office was made with no problems. Sanchez was pleased to find that, as well as the fine money, there were a few hundred bucks left over. Zebulon Pikestaff and his lackeys were so surprised that the fine was being paid that no objections were raised. It was only later that the judge realized that he had been done out of more free labour to work his mine.

Within two hours the released man and his oddball saviour were heading back down the trail. Both were glad to see the back of Deadwood. Black Shadow had been well taken care of in the livery stable. The owner clearly knew and valued good horseflesh. Daggert rewarded his good judgement with a bonus.

The Arab stallion was also eager to prove he still had the legs. Daggert had no need to urge the horse to full speed as Shadow sensed his master's desire to put the inglorious town miles behind them.

11

No Luck in Deadwood

Around the same time as Johnny Daggert was in Deadwood, Buckskin Joe Swann and his buddy Cactus Bob were pulling out of Querida with a packmule in tow. Maggie was outside the diner. The last thing Joe saw before leaving the settlement was the girl's captivating smile. He wanted to turn around, go back and forget about Johnny Daggert. But somehow he managed to return the wave and point his horse's head to the north.

Joe was under no illusions that a delectable girl like Maggie May would not lack for male admirers during the coming months. Hot-blooded young rakes would be more than eager to keep her warm when winter laid its icy hand across the landscape. He thrust the notion aside. Hadn't she said she would wait for him? All he could hope was that she had meant it.

But for now other things had to take priority over his love life.

There was no time to waste if they were to reach Deadwood before Daggert's period for paying his fine expired. Joe knew that vigilante law was extremely fickle. The jiggers who administered it made their own rules on the spot. Stringing a miscreant up to the nearest tree and '*jerking him to Jesus*' could depend on what mood the judge was in at the time.

Major towns like Denver and Laramie had their own official law courts. But many of the distant newly formed boom towns were wide open and lawless. By 1875, large numbers of miners were flooding into the new workings of Blacktail Gulch. All were eager to strike it rich. Deadwood was the main settlement but was still cut off for much of the year by snow blocking access through the mountain passes in winter.

Summer was now well advanced, with aspen leaves starting to turn. Another few weeks and the hillsides would become a riot of bright yellow. Soon after that the town would become inaccessible to all but the hardiest travellers.

Days passed by as the two trackers headed north. They passed through numerous mining camps, including St Elmo, Iron City, Cripple Creek, Anaconda and Gillett. All of them bore evidence of ongoing mining activity. Denver was quickly bypassed to the west. Bad memories from the recent trial were best left behind.

They made much faster progress across the eastern plains of Colorado, after which they entered Nebraska, crossing the North Platte at Scotts Bluff. The well-known landmark on the renowned Oregon Trail had considerable significance for Bob.

'My folks came this way as part of a wagon train back in '52,' he said, staring hard at the rock. 'Soon after, two wagons had to pull out of the column due to an outbreak of cholera. It was on the orders of the leader, so that the disease wouldn't spread. There was no other choice. But it left two families vulnerable to attack from marauding bands of Cheyenne Indians.'

This was the first time that Bob had spoken about his kin before. Joe stayed quiet, allowing his partner to unburden himself in his own good time. Tears welled in the kid's eyes as he recalled the events told to him years later by his mother.

'Ma was the only one to survive, by feigning death. She was picked up by the next train to pass by. They took her on to Fort Laramie, where she stayed for the winter. When spring arrived she managed to get a lift back to Independence. That's where she met my pa.'

'You see much of him?' asked Joe.

'Once in while. He runs a saddle shop back in Omaha.'

For the rest of that day the rain fell in torrents. Talking was out of the question. All their concentration was needed for controlling the horses. The animals were made skittish by the crackles of lightning that forked across the dark sky.

So it was with some relief that they came across a wagon train camped in a hollow to weather out the storm. The conestogas had been drawn round into the traditional circle for protection. Anxiety regarding their reception caused the two trekkers to approach in tense silence. Their hesitation proved to be unjustified when the settlers welcomed the newcomers into their fold without any qualms.

Just as welcoming was the cessation of the storm, which moved off towards the west. The sun quickly emerged from its cocoon of cloud, bathing the landscape in a radiant glow.

It turned out that the travellers were of the Mormon faith and heading for Utah. The two riders were grateful for the offer of home-cooked chow and a rest up for the night. Their wet duds were soon steaming beside a roaring fire. After the evening meal, banjos and fiddles were produced. The singing and dancing offered a welcome respite from their gruelling trek.

That night they enjoyed an undisturbed sleep. All too soon it was over. By first light they were on the trail again, having thanked their kindly hosts for sharing their scarce provisions with two somewhat bedraggled strangers.

Some time later the Black Hills appeared in the distance. A fine veil of mist rose into the grey sky. This region was noted for its damp climate. Once again the pair donned yellow slickers as the steady downpour welcomed them to the territory of South Dakota.

The first building they came across on the southern edge of Deadwood was a single-storey lock-up. Although barely worthy of the name jailhouse, it was of necessity a solid structure, with only one barred window set in the heavy oak door. But there was no adjoining law office.

Passing by, the two riders could hear the muted hollering of voices from inside.

'Looks like that skunk Daggert has company,' observed Joe, offering his partner a mocking smile. He knew the guy only as Derby John Daggert, and that was how it would remain. Abraham Baker was from a different era.

Bob scoffed, aiming a lump of phlegm at the building and its principal tenant.

'You figured how we're gonna play this, Joe?' he asked now that the time for action had finally arrived. 'That critter will not want to walk out of that jail arm in arm with the two jaspers he least wants to see. He's bound to cause a fuss and alert the law as to our intentions.'

'You're right there, Cactus.' They carried on along the street keeping eyes skinned for a sign pointing to the law office. 'I've been giving it some thought myself over the last few days,' Joe added, drawing his horse to a stop. 'The most obvious solution is for us to announce that we're just messengers bringing the fine from Daggert's brother. We can say that we offered to deliver it seeing as we were heading up this way.'

'That's good thinking,' agreed Bob. 'Then we can leave without seeing Daggert but keep a watch for the direction the skunk takes after being released.'

'Simple as falling off'n a log,' added Joe, nudging his tired mount back into motion. The two sidekicks continued along the main street of the town. At least this part of Deadwood seemed to have settled into some semblance of organization. A developing civilization was struggling to assert itself with the familiar establishment of services needed for a predominantly male populace.

As expected, saloons abounded. Then there was the ubiquitous National Hotel, one of which every town in the West seemed to have. They passed a couple of Chinese laundries and a chop house. Tin shops offering the wherewithal to make tools as well as carpenters to build; everything being geared up to serve the mining industry.

Further on up the rutted main street they dodged around piles of detritus that nobody had bothered to shift. Hungry-looking dogs loitered around the butcher's shop, hoping to snap up any scraps.

Suddenly, gunfire erupted from the Raven's Wing saloon a block ahead. Two men backed out of the swing doors, shooting as they emerged. Joe and his partner took cover behind a wagon to watch the outcome of the fracas.

Another two men blundered out of the saloon, returning the fire. None of the shooters succeeded in hitting their targets. All were too severely debilitated by drink. Much hallooing and raucous cussing were all they could manage. But if the rumpus continued, the law of averages meant that blood was sure to be spilled.

A large bulky dude sporting a thick black beard came running out of another saloon called the Black Dog. He fired both barrels of a shotgun into the air.

That instantly quelled the shooting and the vocal clamour from in front of the Raven's Wing.

'If'n it's a set-to you fellas want,' the big man rasped out in a suitably belligerent voice, 'then do it outside of the town limits.' Standing in the middle of the street, legs apart, he quickly jammed fresh cartridges into the barrel of his Greener.

'You know the rules. The vigilance committee don't take kindly to guys causing a shindig. Excepting, of course, on the fourth of July. And that's long since gone.'

The blunt order seemed to sober the quartet up rapidly. Muttering under their breath, the participants holstered their guns and wandered back into the saloon. But one of them stood his ground. Ace Montana was either braver than the rest, or more foolhardy. But the reckless jasper was darned if he was gonna be pushed around any longer. Perhaps he'd had more to drink than the others.

On the spur of the moment he decided to express his opinion on the dubious authority of these self-appointed dispensers of the law.

'I reckon it's about time we had a proper lawman in Deadwood. Somebody appointed by the territorial governor.' He puffed out his scrawny chest and jabbed a finger at the bearded committee man. 'You guys just make it up to suit your own ends. Handing out fines left, right and centre for any damn thing.'

The other men nodded but stepped back, not wishing to buck the only legal representation in the valley.

Joe and his partner remained hidden, fascinated by this unexpected confrontation. Whatever the outcome, they now knew where to deliver the fine money.

The vigilantes must have their headquarters in the Black Dog. And the guy toting a Greener was clearly one of the leading participants. Also, he knew how to use his weapon. Quick as lightning he slotted fresh cartridges into the empty barrels, then snapped the gun shut one-handed with a flick of the wrist.

'So, Montana, you don't like the committee's way of handling things,' drawled the bearded man known as Cracker. It was a statement rather than a question.

'You heard me. And I ain't the only one complaining.'

'Then maybe we ought to do something about your grievance.' Cracker's mordant growl sent a shiver down the backs of the onlookers. Without any further discussion of the matter, the vigilante lifted the lethal firearm. For a second time the gun roared. Black smoke issued from the twin spouts.

Montana was lifted bodily by the force of the blast. He crashed through the front window of the saloon. Slivers of glass showered his *compadres*. Howls of pain from those injured this time were not followed by any objections.

Cracker merely blew the smoke from his gun. Then turned on his heel and returned to the meeting that had so recently been interrupted.

Buckskin Joe and his buddy were stunned by the sudden brutality of the execution carried out before their eyes.

So this was how vigilante law operated in wide open towns. Maybe it was the only way to keep order in these wild places. But Joe couldn't help speculating that the sooner real law came to Deadwood and its counterparts, the better for all concerned. In that respect the dead man had been right. Unfortunately, he had voiced his protest to the wrong person.

'Maybe we need a drink before visiting those vigilante dudes,' suggested Bob nervously. His face had assumed a greenish tinge. The violent incident had shaken him up, bringing home the precarious nature of life in this outpost of the Western frontier.

'I ain't about to disagree with that notion,' said Joe, walking his horse over to the hitching rail in front of the Raven's Wing. The dead man was just being carried over to the undertaker's on the far side of the street.

An hour later, the two buddies summoned up the nerve to head off down to the Black Dog. The bartender had told them to ask for a guy called Zebulon Pikestaff. He was the president and self-appointed judge in Deadwood.

As the two men walked slowly down to the saloon, flakes of snow were drifting down from the grey sky.

'Looks as if winter has arrived early this year,' remarked Joe.

By the time they had reached the door of the Black Dog, the drift had increased to a steady flurry.

Inside, the saloon had the appearance of hundreds of similar establishments catering to the needs of the mining community. There was a rough-hewn bar down one side. Tables were scattered around offering numerous games of chance. In the corner a pianist was belting out a popular song to which men were wildly dancing with each other. Not a single woman was in sight.

At the far end, where a stage had been erected, a man sat on what looked like a throne. Compared to the large ornate chair with its velvet drapes, its occupant was diminutive. So this rather insignificant specimen had to be the bossman of the vigilantes, mused Joe under his breath. The fellow was nattily dressed with a tall beaver-skin hat on his skull-like head, which made him look like a clown.

But nobody laughed at Zebulon Pikestaff.

The eccentric appearance was all an illusion. This guy clearly had power. Behind him stood the implacable Cracker. The executioner acted as Pikestaff's enforcer. Doubtless there were others within easy reach.

Joe couldn't help noticing that both men wore red sashes around their left arms with a similar item serving as a hatband. Numerous other patrons in the saloon sported the same accessory. It was clearly a uniform of some sort.

The meeting appeared to have

ended. Joe sucked in a breath and made his way over to the stage and its bizarre tenant.

'Judge Pikestaff?' he asked in a suitably humble tone. The man just stared down his beaky nose at the intruders. Joe reached into his pocket. On seeing this action the enforcer stiffened. Only when the envelope emerged did he relax, although his piercing black eyes never left the two men.

Joe handed the envelope over, explaining the story they had concocted. Pikestaff heard him out in silence. Once the story had been told, he winked at his associate. The two vigilantes burst out laughing.

A red flush spread across Joe's stubbled cheeks. His jaw tightened. He was becoming a mite irritated by the arrogant disdain displayed by these self-professed overseers of the law. What was so darned funny about paying off a fine?

That was when the judge spoke for the first time.

'Seems like you're a mite too late, friend.' What emerged from between the thin lips was a surprisingly deep and resonant voice for such a pocket-sized figure. A voice that commanded attention. 'The fine was paid off a week ago.'

Now it was Joe and his sidekick's turn to demonstrate a degree of surprise. This was something they had never expected. It also appeared that Johnny Daggert must have teamed up with someone else.

Once he had recovered from the shock Joe voiced his concern.

'Mind telling us if'n they are still in Deadwood? So's we can let his brother know.'

'I don't mind at all,' answered Pikestaff sonorously, lighting up a cigar that looked like a cannon in his small hand. 'My boys made sure they both left town straight away once the dough had been handed over. We don't want their kind causing trouble in this town.' Cracker nodded his agreement.

'It's darned lucky for them both that my associate here didn't ventilate their hides,' Pikestaff added with a raucous laugh.

The kowtowing lackey joined in, eager to please the boss. 'I was out of town at the time,' the enforcer growled out in that unexpectedly gravelly voice. 'Collecting claim rents from the miners.'

The two vigilantes then resumed their conversation, effectively indicating that the brief meeting was over.

Joe waited, expecting Pikestaff to hand back the envelope of greenbacks. But the judge merely slotted the package into the pocket of his blue velvet frock-coat.

'Ain't you forgotten something?' asked the scout sharply.

Pikestaff sniffed. Another imperious look speared the questioner.

'The money!' Joe held out his hand.

The judge stood up. His small stature did nothing to diminish the threatening aura of power surrounding him. An atmosphere of menace had infiltrated the room.

Over near the bar, a large black hound stirred, adding to the growing sense of danger. A feral snarl growled behind bared teeth.

'Consider that to be your contribution for the upkeep of the guy during his stay with us,' smirked the little man. 'Things like that don't come cheap in Deadwood.'

'Why, you scheming son of — ' Joe took a step forward.

Cactus Bob immediately grabbed his *compadre*'s arm before he said anything more that they would both live to regret, or otherwise. The racking back of half a dozen gun hammers to their rear supported the argument for caution.

'Time we was leaving, buddy,' he advised, pulling Joe away. 'These guys mean business. And there are more of them than we can handle.'

'Your friend has spoken a heap of sense, mister,' Pikestaff told him, wagging an admonishing finger in mock rebuke. 'We make the law in Deadwood. And you'd do well to remember that on your way out of town.'

'What the boss means,' cut in the enforcer, brandishing his shotgun, 'is that you have an hour to leave Deadwood. I see you on the street after . . . ' he cast an eye to the ticking clock on the wall, 'five o'clock, you're both dead meat.'

Joe's face flushed a deep purple. His teeth ground in frustration. But he allowed himself to be led away.

Outside, the snow had increased substantially. They could barely see the far side of the street. Their horses were tired, their supplies were exhausted and night was fast approaching. Yet they had less than an hour to leave Deadwood. The situation was grim.

'Best we head back down the trail through Blacktail Gulch and find some place to rest up in one of the outlying camps.'

Cactus Bob's proposal was their best option in the circumstances. 'It shouldn't take more than an hour to reach Central City.'

'Good thinking, Cactus,' said Joe, mounting his horse. 'I noticed there were plenty of empty cabins when we passed. We can figure out our next move come daybreak. I sure don't want to see this place again in a hurry.' He snorted, aiming a glob of spittle at the window of the Black Dog.

In that assertion, both he and Johnny Daggert could agree.

12

The Deadwood Stage

Two days later, they crossed over the territorial boundary into Wyoming by way of Skull Pass. Thereafter, better progress was made across the rolling plains of Thunder Basin. Snow covered the landscape as the temperatures plummeted. The two men were grateful for the sheepskin fleeced jackets and woolly angora chaps to keep them warm. Buckskin was all right for most of the year, but the big freeze demanded more substantial garments.

A keen wind blew across the sagebrush terrain, churning up the loose-packed snow into high drifts that soon became difficult to negotiate. For two days they were forced to seek shelter in a cave. Outside, the wind howled a mournful lament. A leaden sky, heavy with snow, made the difference between night and day almost negligible.

On the third day they awoke to a sparkling firmament of bright blue. The sun reflecting off the gleaming white carpet hurt their eyes. But it was a welcome respite from the blizzards. The rest-up in the cave had done both them and the horses a power of good.

They headed off in a general south-westerly direction, reaching the town of Casper two days later. From there it was but a short ride to Joe's cabin in the shadow of the Laramie Mountains.

In some ways he was glad to be home. Here was as good a place as any to winter down. He was sure that Colonel Mortimer would be eager to have him back on the payroll. On the other hand, it meant at least four months before he would see Maggie May again. A girl like that would only be prepared to wait so long before casting her eye elsewhere.

Not one to fret over what could not be changed, Joe set about gathering in supplies for the winter. He assured Cactus Bob that another scout would always be welcomed by the army, especially in these erratic times when the tribes were on the warpath.

Before reporting back to the commander of Fort Fetterman, Joe visited Casper. It was a centre for the local cattle industry on the banks of the North Platte River. More important was the fact that it had an officially appointed lawman in residence.

Joe was eager to learn if John Daggert had passed through in the last month. Unfortunately, his general description of the guy proved of little help. It could apply to almost anyone. Drifters by the hundred passed through Casper every month. Some were heading north for the gold fields, others looking for work with the cattle outfits.

'I'll keep my eyes and ears open for this dude,' Sheriff Gabe Doolin assured his visitor. 'But I can't promise anything.' Joe had to be satisfied with that.

Life settled down to a habitual pattern as winter tightened its icy grip on the land. The cold was intense and numbing. A fire had to be kept lit at all times to prevent the cabin and its occupants from freezing up in the sub-zero temperatures.

Throughout the territory, almost everything came to a standstill. The citizens of Wyoming and all points north and west hunkered down like hibernating creatures to see out the winter of 1875.

Army patrols were still sent out to check on the outlying settlements and the movement of the Indian tribes. Joe and his partner were vital participants in these forays. But it seemed that Dark Cloud and the other chiefs of the Arapahoe nation had also decided to call time, at least until the following spring. Only hunting parties were spotted as the need for survival in the harsh conditions outweighed the desire for revenge against the hated white invaders.

Joe made a habit of visiting the sheriff's office in Casper twice a month. While collecting supplies, he checked on the current batch of Wanted dodgers pinned up on the notice board. None bore any relation to his quarry. Derby John, it appeared, had also gone to ground for the winter.

At the same time, Joe sent regular wires to Maggie May. Each time he entered the telegraph office the army scout was on tenterhooks when he received a reply. Would this one be a *Dear Joe, I regret* . . . message? But hope springs eternal in the human breast. And on each occasion so far his spirits had been lifted by her equal declarations of commitment.

On leaving the office it always felt like he was walking on a cloud. A stirring euphoria enveloped his whole being. Such sentiments helped get him through the long dark months of winter. Cactus Bob was good company, but . . .

★　★　★

Once winter had finally relaxed its icy grip on the landscape Johnny Daggert was more than ready to get started from where he had left off the previous fall.

The year of 1875 had not been a good one. He firmly intended that 1876 would make up for that, big time.

Daggert blamed his sojourn in that Deadwood hoosegow on his run of bad luck. It was fortunate that his partner had paid off the fine that his no-good brother had refused. Another few days and those bastard vigilantes would have chained him to a wagon in one of the mines. Each time he thought about it, his blood froze.

Daggert cursed aloud. 'Bastard!'

The word was punched out with venom. Sanchez looked up, startled by his partner's oath. But he could read what was churning over in the outlaw's wily brain. Zebulon Pikestaff was going to pay dearly for bucking Johnny Daggert. Then he would go find Aaron. The outlaw promised himself that his miserly brother would regret that knock-back.

He and Sanchez had spent the winter months holed up in a remote boom town that had almost gone bust when the well of plenty ran dry. All that kept the place alive was its remote situation in the heart of the Big Horn Mountains. Known as Mousehole, it attracted outlaws, rustlers and army deserters from far afield. The host of desperadoes were all eager for a place to lie up well beyond the searching tentacles of the law.

Drinking was one of their principal activities. It was during one of these sessions that Daggert confided in his partner the events in Querida and the subsequent trial. He was proud of having bucked the law. And he intended doing so again.

During the winter months Daggert's silky tongue had persuaded two others to join him along with Chico Sanchez.

Blinker Jackman was a gunslinger hailing from Virginia City in Nevada. After a fatal shoot-out, when he had robbed a store, Jackman had fled the territory and found himself holed up here for the winter. Daggert was glad to have an experienced hold-up man willing to join him. Although the guy's constantly flickering eyes took some getting used to.

The other man was a failed prospector who had solid reasons of his own for getting even with the vigilantes. Genesis Buckhorn was a good ten years older than Daggert. His black hair was streaked with grey and eyes like those of a polecat peered from beneath beetling brows. The guy had a permanent scowl plastered across his angular face, the result of a knife-fight some years earlier.

Buckhorn had naïvely borrowed money off Pikestaff to finance his claim along a side valley called Bear Butte Canyon. When the claim failed to deliver Pikestaff called in the loan. Unable to pay, Buckhorn was forced to work it off on the judge's chain gang. He was more than willing to explain all the grisly details of the vigilante leader's method of payment.

'That was three months of hell,' the ex-miner cursed. 'Let me join you, boys, and I can tell you how to stitch that bastard up good and proper.'

Daggert was all ears. They were gathered round the pot-bellied stove in the middle of the Hell's Acre saloon.

'I couldn't do it alone,' said Buckhorn. 'But four of us should have no trouble.'

'What's this plan you have in mind, Gene?' Daggert asked.

'The regular miners employed at the White Owl and Savoy mines couldn't be paid during the winter because the dough had to be brought in from Pine Ridge. That's on the far side of the badlands.' Buckhorn eased back into his chair. He paused to light a pipe, stoking up the tobacco to his satisfaction before continuing.

Daggert bridled. Patience was not one of his virtues. And this was his gang.

'Hurry it up, mister,' he snapped. 'We ain't got all day.'

184

The harsh tone oozed authority. Daggert had never taken kindly to being given orders, or kept waiting. He liked to be the one in command. The burly ex-miner recognized these facts and immediately began pouring out his scheme.

According to Buckhorn, the first Deadwood stagecoach to come through the mountains after the spring thaw would be carrying the mine-workers' payroll. The money accrued over the winter months would make a lucrative haul for the right gang. Johnny Daggert reckoned that he and his new outfit of villains were more than equal to the task.

As a result of Buckhorn's suggestion, that was to be the gang's first caper. So as not to be late, the line of riders set out from Mousehole at the end of March.

In contrast to the mist-shrouded Black Hills, the badlands was a brutally arid terrain where little rain fell. The hostile, rocky landscape was a sudden and dramatic contrast to Eastern green plains. Ancient riverbeds had long since disappeared. Only the hardiest of vegetation managed to secure a toehold here. Amidst the heavy alkaline crusts, only tough thorn-bushes, mesquite and cholla cactus survived.

Into this pitiless environment Johnny Daggert led his men. He was astute enough to allow Genesis Buckhorn to take over heading the small column when they entered the badlands proper. Buckhorn knew this unforgiving land better than any of them. Daggert had promised him an increased share of the haul for his valuable contribution.

After crossing the shallows of Battle Creek, the gang entered the forbidding wilderness. Buckhorn led them a meandering course through steep-sided canyons and across stretches of grey ash. No hesitation was noticeable from the stiff back of the ageing owlhoot, who seemed to know exactly where he was headed.

Daggert was less certain. How could anybody find their way through this wasteland?

'You ain't leading us into the Devil's Kitchen are you, Gene?' he called out from behind.

'Trust me, boss,' came back the confident response. 'Just another mile and we'll be at the perfect spot for an ambush.'

So it proved. Sturgis Cutting was a narrow ravine, wide enough for a stagecoach to pass through but with boulders on either side providing cover. It was a bleak and lonely place. Ideal for a robbery.

Daggert smiled. That skunk Zebulon Pikestaff was going to suffer where it hurt the most: in his pocket.

He slapped his confederate on the back. 'Never doubted you for a minute. You done well, Gene.' The older man accepted the praise like a strutting rooster. 'How long before the stage comes along, d'yuh reckon?' Daggert enquired.

Buckhorn took his timing from the sun's height in the azure sky. 'I figure we've got another couple of hours before it's due. That is so long as they keep to the regular schedule that they operated last year.'

'Time enough for a final smoke. Then we can settle in.' Addressing the others, Daggert gave his orders for where each participant was to position himself for the best advantage. His last order was addressed to the Nevada hardcase.

'Blinker, you get up on that ledge. Give us the signal when you see the coach coming. And no smoking up there. We don't want to give them any advance warning.'

'Sure thing, boss.'

Like the other members of the gang, the gunslinger knew that Derby John held a royal flush in this deal. He moved off without a murmur of dissent.

Time passed slowly, the mesmeric golden orb struggling across the bright blue of the heavens. With an effort, Johnny suppressed his impatience. He passed the time by checking his hardware.

At last the signal from Jackman told him all he needed to know.

'On your feet, boys,' he rapped out. 'Take up your positions. And no shooting until I give the word.'

Ten minutes later the thudding of cantering hoofs accompanied by the rattle of the coach reached his ears. Muscles tensed. Brief nods were passed between the waiting outlaws, clenched hands tightly grasping their weapons. When the jouncing Concord came into view, Daggert lined up the sights of his rifle on the guard sitting atop the coach, next to the driver.

Without any hesitation he loosed off a single shot. The man grasped at his shoulder where the bullet had struck. His shotgun disappeared under the wheels of the coach. He slumped over and would have disappeared along with the gun had not the driver grabbed his arm.

'Haul up, driver, else the next bullet has your name on it.' The blunt order immediately caused the driver to wrestle one-handed with the leathers, bringing the coach to a juddering halt.

Daggert and his men jumped out from their places of concealment, guns bristling with menace.

'All we want is the strongbox containing the dough,' shouted Daggert, waving his gun. 'No trouble and you can be on your way.'

Before the driver could respond a face appeared in the window of the coach.

'What in thunder is going on here?'

'Well I'll be darned!' exclaimed Daggert, his face splitting in a hideous grin. 'If'n that don't beat all. Mister Jubilee Cracker!' The mirthless leer instantly dissolved, to be replaced by a far more intimidating growl. 'Get out of there real slow so's I can see your worthless hide.'

'Who are you?' asked the nervous bodyguard.

'You don't recognize me, ugh?' Without waiting for a reply Daggert addressed his next order to the gang. 'Chico, you watch these guys while Blinker and Gene grab the dough and transfer it to our saddle-bags. I've gotten me some unfinished business with Mr Cracker here.'

With no further ado the gang boss slugged the bodyguard in the mouth with a bunched fist. Cracker went down in a heap, blood pouring from the mashed orifice.

'Get up,' snarled Daggert, eager to continue with the punishment. 'I'm one of the poor saps you locked up in that stinking jail of yourn. It was my buddy here that paid off the fine.' He nodded to Sanchez while clenching his hands ready to deliver another flurry of bone-crunching blows to that hated visage.

But at that very moment, the unmistakable sound of hoofs assailed his ears. There was more than one rider, and they were coming from the same direction as the coach had been travelling. Was this a trap, an escort to thwart a robbery? Or maybe it was just bad luck that another group of riders were heading that way.

Daggert had no intention of hanging around to find out.

He whistled for Black Shadow to join him. The faithful horse dutifully trotted round from behind the rocks where he had been secreted.

'You got the dough, Blinker?' he shouted while mounting up.

'Sure have, boss,' came back the spirited cry.

'Then let's ride!'

The robbers swung their horses westerly and bounded off up the winding ravine.

At that moment two riders hove into view. Judging by their appearance they were merely prospectors heading for the goldfields.

Unfortunately for Sanchez, his corpulent girth proved a hindrance to swift movement. He was still struggling to mount up when Cracker managed to shake off the mush from his recent pummelling. The vigilante pulled out his pistol and fired.

The 'breed's ample size made for an

easy target. Two bullets pursued him as he made to escape. One struck him in the leg, the other plucked at his arm. He tumbled out of the saddle. Sanchez was not badly hurt, but with a slug in his leg he was unable to walk.

'Help me, Johnny!' he yelped in pain, waving his good arm in panic. 'I am hit. You cannot leave Sanchez here.'

Daggert looked back. But his pace slackened only momentarily. 'Too bad, Chico. But we ain't stopping for no shoot-out. You'll have to take your chance with the vigilantes. Good luck, you'll need it. But we'll make certain to spend your share of the loot wisely.'

With that parting witticism the three outlaws disappeared in a cloud of dust. Bullets pursued them, pinging off the surrounding rocks, but they went well wide.

13

Red for Danger

It was mid-afternoon in Casper. Buckskin Joe Swann was enjoying a cup of coffee and a slice of apple pie in the Sweetwater Café. The snack was made all the more palatable due to the letter he had just received from Maggie May.

A wistful expression cloaked his rugged face as he avidly devoured both cake and letter contents. Halcyon images, made all the more poignant by time and distance floated before him. All his dreams involved intimacies to which only he could be privy. It was now over six months since he had last seen her. A lifetime for a young man in the throes of his first true romance. The yearnings that tugged at his heartstrings elicited a series of deep lugubrious sighs.

Would he ever catch up with Derby John Daggert?

His doleful attitude was invaded by a tap on the shoulder. It was Cactus Bob. The kid pushed a newspaper under his associate's nose.

'Read this,' he snapped out, excitedly jabbing a finger at the article in question. 'Could be that we've got a breakthrough in our search for Daggert.'

This news brought Joe tumbling out of his morose demeanour. He quickly scanned the important passage. It appeared that a robbery had taken place in the Badlands of South Dakota in which a payroll had been stolen. Four men had been involved, one of whom had been captured and was now awaiting trial by the miners' court in Deadwood. Judge Zebulon Pikestaff would be presiding.

Joe was losing patience. 'What's this got to do with Daggert?' he demanded.

'Just read on and you'll see,' Cactus insisted.

Joe's gaping peepers eagerly perused the rest of the article.

Then he saw it. The guy in the lock-up was described as a half-breed Mexican by the name of Chico Sanchez. That name certainly made Joe sit up. The 'breed had spilled the beans, naming Daggert as the leader of the gang to save his own skin.

Joe shot a look at his partner.

'This sure is a lucky break,' Cactus iterated, reading his buddy's mind. 'He and the others managed to escape with the money. But that 'breed you chased out of Wild Horse Gulch knows where they'll be holed up.'

'If'n we can somehow find a way of securing Sanchez's freedom, he could lead us to the varmint,' said Joe, his entire being suddenly animated. Here was their chance to finally bring the killer to justice. According to the reporter, the vigilante trial had been a formality. Sanchez had been found guilty of robbery and sentenced to work on the judge's chain gang. He was due to be taken up to serve his sentence in the Savoy mine the following week.

The chief problem was how to separate Sanchez from the vigilante gang's clutches. 'You got any ideas, Bob?' Joe asked his partner.

The younger man considered the question for a moment. Then his youthful features lit up in a smile of enlightenment. He snapped his fingers.

'You remember those guys all wore red sashes as a mark of their association with the vigilantes?'

Joe responded with a slow nod.

'If'n we can get a-hold of some red material, maybe we could fool them into accepting us as members of their gang.'

Joe slapped his partner on the back. 'Good thinking, buddy. All we need is to get close enough to surprise them. Our guns can do the talking after that.'

'Sally Ann Stoker across the street runs a dress shop,' said Bob. 'I'm sure she will have some suitable material.'

'That's the girl you're sweet on, ain't

it?' Joe smiled. Now it was Bob's turn to blush. His face assumed the radiant hue of a late sunset.

To save his associate any further embarrassment, Joe hurried on: 'In that case, we better get started if'n we're to reach Deadwood in time. You sort out the sashes while I buy in supplies.'

Stuffing the last of the apple pie into his mouth, he quickly paid his bill and the pair departed. After securing the all-important red sashes from the dressmaker they headed back to the cabin to collect their gear. On the way they called at Fort Fetterman to inform Colonel Mortimer of their need for more time off. As always, the officer was sympathetic to their cause. He wished them every success in their quest for justice.

A couple of hours later they were heading back across Thunder Basin towards the Black Hills.

On reaching Blacktail Gulch, they once again took advantage of the cabin they had previously occupied, which was still empty. Surreptitious enquiries in Central City elicited the information that the prisoners, of which there were three, were being escorted to the Savoy mine in two days.

Their interest in Sanchez did not require any probing. Talk of the half-breed's fate was on everybody's lips. It was no secret that he had suffered at the hands of the vigilantes. Pikestaff was livid when he heard about the robbery.

When asked about the vigilante leader's reaction, one old guy who had been in Deadwood at the time couldn't contain his mirth.

'Jumped about like a one-legged turkey he did. That sure was a sight to behold.'

The others joined in the laughter. Most of the miners in Central City sympathized with the captured robber. Judge Pikestaff and his bunch were not well-regarded in the valley. They had far too much power. Joe and his buddy readily concurred with that declaration.

But Pikestaff's men, led by the bestial Cracker, had taken brutal retribution against the unfortunate captive. He had been kept alive solely to labour in the Savoy mine. What would happen afterwards did not bear thinking about.

Maintaining a low profile, the two friends settled down to wait.

On the appointed day they were up at the crack of dawn. There was no knowing at what hour the prisoners would be leaving the Deadwood lock-up. To avoid being recognized by any of Pikestaff's bully boys, they made a circuitous trail around the town. Climbing up through the array of tree stumps that covered the valley slopes, they picked a course that took advantage of any opportunities for concealment.

On the far side of the town they descended to valley level. A clear trail headed west into the narrow gorge of Spearfish Creek. Reports that they gleaned in Central City suggested this was the direction the prisoners and escort would take. As they climbed steadily through the ranks of ponderosa pine and spruce, any indication of human presence was soon left behind.

'Keep your eyes peeled for a good spot to make our play,' Joe advised his partner. 'We don't want to give them any room for manoeuvring.'

They settled for a place where the trail began to rise quite steeply. Horses would be forced down to a walk in single file. The dense network of trees on either side provided adequate cover. Over the next hour they worked out a plan of campaign. The elevated position they had chosen offered a fine view down the gorge, enabling the watchers to observe the approach of their quarry well in advance.

It was late morning when they sighted the line of riders snaking up the twisting trail beside Crazy Woman Falls. The noise was deafening. The rushing waters of the cataract were swollen by the spring thaw higher up in the mountains.

'Time to slip on our disguises,' said

Joe, fixing a red sash around his hatband and another on to the left sleeve of his shirt. Cactus did likewise. Both men pulled their hats down to hide their faces. 'Those critters will think you're a late arrival when you call out to them from behind. That will give me the chance to get the drop on them from up front.'

'Do we offer them the chance to surrender?' Bob asked, not that he was over bothered about the niceties of fair combat where these skunks were concerned.

'I'll order them to shed their weapons,' replied Joe. 'Odds on they'll resist. But the advantage will be with us.'

Bob swallowed nervously. There was no doubting that he was feeling the strain. Joe recognized the kid's anxiety. So he tried to calm his buddy's nerves.

'When they swing round in the saddle, the sun will be in their eyes. That'll give you the edge, kid. Remember all that shooting practice we put in back of Jubal Kade's gun shop?' Another tentative nod from Cactus Bob. 'Well here's your chance to do it for real. So make every bullet count. I ain't got no doubts that you can do it. And don't forget to wear your spectacles,' he added.

Bob's reply was blunt: 'I dumped them darned things after that hoohaw in the Denver courtroom. That lawyer made me look a right lame brain.'

'You sure ain't no limp biscuit, Cactus. I wouldn't have brought you along if'n I couldn't trust you to play your part.'

A warm smile and squeeze of the arm gave the young man back his confidence. And he needed it. When it came to the crunch, this was the first time he had been involved in a real gun battle.

The line of riders had slowed to a walk as they began the slow pull up the steep gradient alongside the Spearfish. The rotund figure of Chico Sanchez was unmistakable in the middle of the group. Even from that distance Joe could see that the Mexican had suffered at the hands of the vigilantes. He scowled, then swung his horse round, secreting himself in the trees higher up the trail.

Bob did likewise further down, just below a sharp bend in the trail. There he waited. Sweat dribbled down his face even though the temperature up here in the rocky wilderness was barely above freezing. Snow still cloaked the upper ridges of the mountain range. A glistening halo of spring sunshine was lost on the young man as he listened intently for the sound of approaching hoofbeats.

Minutes passed; they seemed like hours to the waiting ambushers.

At last the rattle of harness and creaking of leather announced the imminent arrival of the prisoners and their escort. A minute later the column passed by close to where Cactus Bob was hidden. Two red sashes were in the lead followed by the three prisoners, with another three guards bringing up the rear.

Bob gave them the chance to pass around the bend up ahead before he pulled out and urged his horse up the grade.

'Hold up there, you guys!' he called out from behind the column. 'Wait for me.'

The riders drew to a stop. The rear guards turned around in their saddles, hands reaching for holstered pistols. When they saw the red sashes on the newcomer's hat and arm their postures visibly relaxed.

'What you doing up here?' asked one of the guards.

'The boss sent me to join you,' Bob said in a punchy voice. 'He thought you could do with some extra help.'

'Ain't seen you around before,' the other guard butted in, suspicious. He shielded the eastern sun out of his eyes, moving closer to get a better look at the new man.

'What's happening back there?' shouted one of the front guards.

It was Cracker.

Bob instantly recognized the brutish snarl in the bodyguard's tone. Cracker had turned his horse around and was nudging down the grade to intervene. Bob stiffened in the saddle. The hardcase would surely recall the black-haired young guy from the previous fall, when they had come to Deadwood to pay off that fine on the varmint who had already flown the coop.

Buckskin Joe had also taken heed of the bodyguard and decided it was time to make his presence felt.

'Put your hands in the air,' he snapped out tersely. 'Anybody reaches for a gun and he'll be dancing with the Devil.'

All the guards immediately swung back to face this new threat from up the trail. For a brief moment nobody moved. A buzzard cawed. Then, as Joe had expected, Cracker went for his gun. The others immediately followed his lead.

'Let 'em have it, Bob!' Joe screamed out. Pistol already to hand, he pumped lead at the milling guards.

The guards' shock at being ambushed

gave the attackers the element of surprise, of which they took full advantage. When the guards turned to face Joe, Cactus had palmed his own revolver ready for action.

Once the showdown had started, any nervous trepidation left him. He was immediately caught up in the adreneline-pumping tension of battle. Blood pumped through his veins. Again and again the Navy Colt bucked in his hand. When it clicked on empty, he discarded it and drew a spare one from his belt.

Horses milled about on the narrow trail, making accurate shooting impossible.

Joe had concentrated on dropping Cracker as soon as he saw that the skunk was going to resist. He rightly assumed that the violent tough was in charge and was the most dangerous of the bunch. Care was needed, however, to avoid hitting the prisoners.

The gunfight lasted barely more than two minutes. In that time three of the guards including Cracker had been killed. Another had been wounded. The lone uninjured survivor tried to retaliate, but soon grasped that he had been outmanoeuvred in the well coordinated ambush.

'OK, mister, you win,' the guard called out, raising his hands and throwing down his gun. 'Don't shoot me.'

Once the fight was clearly over, Joe called for his partner to join him.

The three prisoners were stunned by the sudden shift in their fortunes. They just sat on their horses, mesmerized, unable to comprehend their good luck. One minute they'd been heading for a miserable existence on a chain gang, the next they were free as birds.

'Is this for real?' one of them asked eventually, holding his tethered hands out. 'Are you going to release us?'

Joe didn't reply. His first priority was to secure and tether the two guards. One of the red sashes easily stanched the flesh wound of the injured man. Meanwhile, Bob kept his gun trained on the three prisoners. His stern look did not bode well. Their elation at being released dissolved as quickly as it had arisen.

Having ensured that the guards were no longer any threat, Joe sauntered over to the anxious trio. He cast a searching gaze over the taut faces, a half-smile forming across his craggy features.

'Two of you can go,' he declared, extracting a knife and slicing through the ropes of the selected pair. A flick of his head indicated for the two lucky jiggers to depart. They did not demur. Soon they had disappeared back down the trail in a cloud of dust. Joe's eyes then focused on the third man.

14

Sanchez Comes Good

Chico Sanchez was quaking in his boots. His face was a blotchy mass of cuts and bruises. One eye was swollen shut. But in the other recognition dawned.

'S-señor S-Swann,' he stammered out. 'This is a s-sur-prise. Sanchez not expect to s-see you again so s-soon.'

'I'll bet you didn't,' Joe rapped out. He was in no mood for pussy-footing around. 'For some inexplicable reason you've joined up with Johnny Daggert and his gang. That's the only reason I've saved you from a fate worse than death.'

'And for that I am in your debt, señor.'

'Indeed you are. And you're going to repay that debt by telling me where the skunk is holed up so's I can kill him.' Joe's eyes blazed with fury as he hissed out the demand.

'And I'll be there right beside you to finish the job,' added an equally forthright Cactus Bob. Two gun barrels wavered menacingly in front of the half-breed's quivering body.

Realization that his rescuers were on a mission he himself would most definitely like to join, Sanchez relaxed. He sighed with relief.

'*Señores*, it will be my pleasure to conduct you to the hideout. It is in the Big Horn Mountains, at a place called Mousehole.'

Now it was Joe's turn to register surprise.

Sanchez went on to explain the circumstances that had led to him teaming up with Derby John Daggert. He had been more than willing to help pull a successful heist against the Deadwood vigilantes. But when Daggert had so callously left him to face their wrath after being wounded in the hold-up,

Chico was now eager to see him brought to heel.

'That *bastardo* thought it huge joke to leave poor self to face wrath of vigilantes.' Sanchez was now fully riled up. His corpulent frame shook with anger. 'For that he pay dearly.'

As they were preparing to depart for the Big Horns, Sanchez suggested they search the guards and their mounts for any loot.

'We ain't thieves,' warned Joe. 'So we'll take only what is our due. Two hundred bucks stolen from us, plus maybe another fifty for all our trouble. What about you?' he asked of the portly Mexican.

'I will settle for money I was forced to pay out to secure Daggert's release from the Deadwood lock-up. It also was two hundred.' He purposely omitted to mention how he had come by the money. 'Perhaps when we catch up with that *hombre traidor* you will not begrudge this poor *mestizo* a share of the vigilante money.'

Joe did not reply. It had after all been going to pay the legitimate wages of the miners employed in Pikestaff's Mines.

Instead he stated the problem that was uppermost in his mind. 'I hear that Mousehole is a hard place to find. No lawman has yet managed to penetrate the Big Horns to find it.'

Sanchez didn't get the chance to enlighten him. They were about to depart when the remaining guard called out to them.

'You guys ain't gonna leave me here, are you?' he whined. 'Pikestaff will have me chained to one his wagons for allowing this to happen. I might as well have been gunned down with the others.'

Sanchez aimed a goblet of phlegm at the frightened captive. 'We can always arrange that, *hombre*,' he rasped raising his pistol. 'You were ready enough to make me and my fellow prisoners suffer up there.' A pudgy thumb indicated the trail ahead. 'Now you get some of own medicine.'

Buckskin laid a restraining hand on

the Mexican's arm. He was feeling more benevolent. Frisco De Vere's money had been recovered, plus some extra. In addition they had rescued the guy who could lead them to Daggert, and they'd effectively kicked Zebulon Pikestaff in the teeth.

Altogether a good morning's work.

Beneath the dark beard the guard's face was white with terror. But seeing the leader of the ambushers hesitating, the man pressed his case.

'Let me go and I'll disappear. You won't see me around here again. That's a promise.'

Joe considered for a moment. 'OK, mister, you've caught me in a good mood.' He reached down and cut through the ropes binding the prisoner. 'But I'll keep your hardware, just in case you change your mind.' He pointed the gun at the guy's stomach. 'Understand me?'

The grateful man nodded vigorously, then leapt on to his horse and spurred off.

'You are too kind, Señor Joe,'

exclaimed Sanchez. 'He not deserve any mercy.'

'A guy that bears grudges will never be happy in his own skin.' He threw a mischievous look at the Mexican. 'You think on that, Chico. And you might also recall that I did the same for you once.'

The fat man responded with a knowing smile.

For the rest of that day, with Sanchez in the lead, they headed up the steep trail branching west above the tree line to reach the Wyoming border at Buffalo Gap. This was the route that Daggert and Sanchez had taken when they first arrived in the Black Hills.

They stopped to make camp early because Sanchez complained that his injured leg was aching. Once rested, he limped about the camp preparing the evening meal. A deer-meat stew was soon bubbling in a skillet. And it smelt delicious.

Cooking was a job the jovial Mexican enjoyed. And it was obvious that he also relished his own creations. The culinary task was accompanied by a lilting Mexican love song. Surprisingly, the guy had a melodic voice that was easy on the ear. Joe lit up a cigar, then settled down beside the fire to listen.

The fat guy was unexpectedly proving to be something of an asset.

Once again Joe's thoughts drifted towards the comely image of the lovely Maggie May Joplin. But Chico's song only served to make him more homesick for her company. Accordingly he forced himself to concentrate on the job in hand.

A doubt had been gnawing at his craw all day. Only when Sanchez paused to stir up the stew did he voice his concerns.

'If'n this Mousehole berg is so all-fired safe and hard to locate, how come you're so confident of being able to find the way?' he asked.

'Remember, *señor*, that Sanchez is half Apache,' Sanchez replied, while stirring the pot. 'My father Ojo Caliente taught me how to study and remember the land, so making it work to my advantage. Easy to follow sign when you have had such a teacher.'

Joe was impressed.

Sanchez eyed his associate with a meditative regard. 'I was sorry to hear about your papa, Joe. That real bad thing Daggert did.'

Joe sat up. 'How do you know about that?' he asked sharply.

'He let it slip during the winter. The drink had loosened his tongue.'

Joe's mouth tightened. A hard gleam replaced the soft glow of moments before. Now he had proof that Derby John Daggert was indeed the killer. He'd always known deep down. But learning of the killer's admission put the final nail in his coffin. It was also a momentous revelation that his horse had been instrumental in securing the alibi that led to his acquittal.

★ ★ ★

Four days later they crested a knoll to find the tiny settlement of Mousehole ensconced in the valley below. Joe peered back the way they had come. It seemed little more than a miracle that that they had managed to arrive at their destination so quickly. After experiencing the tortuous route over ridgebacks, across creeks and dried-up riverbeds, through forests and narrow ravines, he could readily see why the law had thus far been denied access to the outlaw stronghold.

It was a veritable labyrinth that would trap the unwary and lead to an untimely demise. Doubtless there were many human remains littering the area of those who had tried and failed to penetrate the Big Horns. Picked clean by wandering scavengers, they would stay unclaimed for eternity.

'Will Daggert be down there now?' Joe enquired.

Sanchez shook his head. 'He has taken over a cabin up a blind draw five miles to the west. The plan was to rest up for a spell before splitting the loot. All being well, he will be at the cabin now.'

'Then we ain't got no time to lose,' announced Joe. He gestured for the Mexican to lead off. 'Once we have established that he and the others are still there, we can plan our next move.'

Sanchez led the way, skirting around the cluster of hutments to avoid being spotted by curious eyes. On reaching the blind draw which they hoped was sheltering the three outlaws, Joe signalled a halt.

'How far up is the cabin?' he asked Sanchez.

'No more than fifteen minutes on foot,' came back the whispered reply.

'Then I suggest we leave our horses here and make our way in there,' Joe said, dismounting. 'Once I get the lie of the land we can decide how best to flush them out.'

After ground hitching the animals they moved cautiously up the sloping bed of the draw. Their guns drawn, their sharp eyes swept the uneven landscape, probing every nook and cranny. Joe had also brought his bow and a quiver of arrows, which were slung over his shoulder.

It was a tense period. Being so close to their quarry was nerve-racking for them all. After the stated fifteen minutes, Sanchez whispered that the cabin was in a glade up ahead, beyond a cluster of rocks.

Not a sound was made as the three pursuers edged gingerly around the rocks. Sanchez removed his trademark sombrero. For a rotund man he was surprisingly nimble on his feet, another trait of his Apache heritage. He moved forward and peered through a gap. A sigh of relief escaped from between his fleshy lips.

'*Madre de Dios!*' he exclaimed breathing deeply. 'They are still there.'

The others joined him. Three horses were lined up outside the cabin, indicating that the outlaws were inside. Smoke drifted up into the sky from a stovepipe on the roof. The small wooden shack backed on to a sheer cliff face. The only way to approach it was from the front.

Sooner or later, one of the cabin's residents would have to come outside. Either to fill a bucket at the well, feed the horses or to relieve himself. That was when Joe intended to make his move. Until then, it was a question of waiting and trusting that what he had in mind would come to fruition.

The sun traced a gradual course across the blue sky. In three hours daylight would begin to fade. That would spell the end of their quest for this day at least. If that happened, the next day could find the gang had slipped away during the night. Split three ways, there would be enough dough to keep them in luxury for quite a spell.

Joe could not bear the thought of that. He was restive, his nerve ends screamed. An arrow was notched in the bow ready to do its duty. All that was needed now was a suitable live target.

Then the moment for which they had been waiting occurred.

15

Draw to a Close

A man had emerged from the cabin. He was a burly jasper wearing a broad-brimmed grey Stetson.

'That is Blinker Jackman,' Sanchez whispered in Joe's ear. 'He one mean-eyed gringo. I saw him shoot a man down in Mousehole for wearing a feather in his hat. Claimed the guy was an Indian-lover.'

Jackman stretched his arms, then sauntered across to a group of bushes.

'He taking a leak,' observed Sanchez.

'When he comes out, I'll be ready for him,' Joe whispered back.

He sucked in a deep breath to steady himself. Slowly he drew back the sturdy ash longbow and sighted along the arrow shaft. To his left, Cactus had his rifle trained in the same direction as a

223

back-up in case Joe missed.

After what seemed a long age, Jackman emerged from the makeshift latrine. Joe waited for him to pause and fasten up his trousers. Then he released the pressure on the bowstring. The arrow shot off with a distinct twang, homing in on its target. All three watched the graceful trajectory as the lethal barb winged its way across the open sward. It struck Jackman in the chest. A perfect hit. The guy threw his arms in the air as a spout of blood erupted from the deadly wound.

Not a sound was uttered as he slowly sank to his knees before keeling over.

Joe smiled. 'You're not the only one to be granted the honour of having an Indian instructor. Mine was Dark Cloud, chief of the eastern Arapahoe before he went hostile.'

'Good shooting,' Cactus Bob praised his partner. 'And not a sound to alert the other two inside the cabin.'

'Sooner or later they are going to wonder what's happened to their sidekick,' Joe remarked, slotting another arrow into the bow. 'Let's hope I can take the next one out just as easily.'

Ten minutes passed before the cabin door opened. A gruff voice shouted, 'What's keeping you, Blinker? Can't you find that pecker of yourn?'

There was no answer. Another man stepped outside. He was much older and more grizzled.

'That is Genesis Buckhorn.' Once again Sanchez provided enlightenment. 'He was a miner who fell foul of Pikestaff and ended up on his chain gang. It would be wrong, I think, to kill him. He a good fellow.'

Joe eyed his associate askance. The Mexican's observation put him in something of a quandary. He only wanted Daggert. This guy was not a real outlaw. Just a guy who appeared to have joined the gang seeking revenge on another rat.

Before he could decide what action to adopt, the decision was taken out of his hands. Buckhorn spotted the arrow in the dead body of Blinker Jackman and assumed the cabin was under attack.

'Indians!' he yelled out, drawing his pistol and firing randomly at the surrounding rocks. Even though there was no target to aim at, he didn't stop until the gun was empty. Some of the shots came close to where the three hunters were secreted, forcing them to duck down. In the meantime Buckhorn had disappeared back into the cabin.

Disturbed by the sudden flurry of pistol shots, a flight of birds rose into the air. Chirping and scudding about, they flew off in search of a more tranquil place to settle. Gunsmoke hung in the static air as silence once again descended on the deceptively peaceful haven.

But it was all an illusion. Violence would be the inevitable outcome of the bout of random gunplay. Joe was certain that Daggert would not surrender without a fight. All he could do now was negotiate with the varmint and hope that he would see reason and release the old-timer from his obligation.

Inside the cabin Johnny Daggert was nonplussed. There hadn't been a sighting of Indians in the valley for some considerable time. The only thing resembling an Indian had been the critter whom Blinker Jackson had gunned down. And he was just some dude who liked wearing feathers in his hat. It had been a foible more than enough to raise the Nevada gunslinger's hackles.

'You sure those critters out there are Indians?' Daggert snapped out at his colleague.

'All I know is that an arrow was poking out of Blinker's chest,' Buckhorn insisted with vigour. 'Who else is likely to be toting a bow in these parts?'

Daggert peered out of the window. Nothing moved. If Indians were out there, why had the red devils not attacked? That was their normal practice. Whooping and hollering with frontal charges.

Then he saw a movement in the rocks at the far side of the clearing. Bringing his Winchester up, he snapped off a couple of shots.

'That'll bring 'em out,' he rasped nervously.

One of the shots had parted Cactus Bob's hair, removing a lump of skin from his scalp. It was not a killing shot, but the kid would not be taking any further part in the shindig about to erupt. Joe made his decision.

Without revealing himself he called out, 'I know you're in there, Daggert. This is Buckskin Joe Swann speaking. And I'm here to take you back to hang for shooting my pa, or to finish the job here myself. It's your choice.'

Daggert stiffened. Joe Swann! So old Israel had a son. How had the critter found him? As if in answer to his unspoken query, Chico Sanchez piped up.

'You should never have abandoned me, Johnny. I saved your hide in that ravine. The least you could have done was help me out when I needed it.'

'So what's it gonna be, Daggert?' Joe called out. 'Die now or at the end of a rope?'

Another two shots were the killer's answer. The bullets zipped and whined off the rocks. But none came near the hidden men.

'I hear you, Johnny,' replied Joe. 'But why not let the old dude go free. This fracas is between you and me now. Let him go and it is sure to go down well with a jury. Maybe even get you a lighter sentence.'

In the cabin raised voices could be heard. Old Genesis Buckhorn was clearly urging his boss to let him go. But Daggert clearly had other ideas. Suddenly the door of the cabin flew open and the old guy burst out. He ran down the slope like an antelope, sheer panic lending him extra speed. He'd almost made the cover of the rocks where Joe and his buddies were concealed when a single rifle shot took him down. Another sealed his fate as the poor sap lay squirming on the ground in a pool of his own blood.

'That's what happens to quitters. You hear me, Swann? And that's what you and your scummy friends will get if'n you try rushing me. I have plenty of supplies in here. What do you have?' A harsh laugh echoed around the draw.

'We have time on our side, Daggert. You stay there if'n you want to. I'm sending Sanchez over to Casper to get a posse. You know he can lead them right here. There'll be a lot of volunteers itching to be the members of the first posse to find Mousehole. Me and my pards will stick around to make sure you don't get lonesome.'

Joe ceased talking to give the outlaw time to reflect. Then he added, 'Surrender to me now and I can make a deal with the law to go easy on you. It'll mean a spell in jail. But that's better than a necktie party. What d'you say?'

Minutes passed. Then a rifle and two revolvers were thrown out of the window.

'OK. Hold your fire. I'm coming out.'

The door opened and Johnny Daggert emerged, arms reaching skywards. Joe was suspicious that the outlaw had given in so easily. He allowed the killer to step into the open before revealing himself. Sanchez joined him as they moved up the shallow rise, ever watchful for any sign of a double cross.

They had almost reached the corral beside the cabin when Daggert pursed his lips and blew a sharp whistle. Joe halted, uncertain what the guy was up to. He was given no time to speculate further, as a pounding of hoofs broke out behind him. Turning, he just had time to see a black horse galloping hell for leather straight at him. Pushing Sanchez to one side, Joe dived to the other. Nevertheless, the animal caught him a stunning blow as it passed.

Before either man had chance to recover his senses, Daggert had leapt on to the back of Black Shadow and was galloping off down the draw. Rider and horse passed the rocks below the cabin and looked certain to escape.

Then a deep boom rang out. The noise of the rifle crack echoed around the draw. Daggert threw up his hands and tumbled from the saddle. Moments later, the swaying form of Cactus Bob staggered out from where he had been lying. The rifle in his hands was smoking.

★   ★   ★

Three days later a trio of riders walked their mounts down the main street of Casper. Each rider was leading another horse with a body draped across the saddle. Cactus had an expertly fashioned bandage around his head, courtesy of the multi-talented skills of Chico Sanchez.

After delivering the bodies to the local undertaker, Joe apprised Sheriff Doolin of the events leading to their current state of lifelessness. The lawman knew about Johnny Daggert's activities and even had a Wanted poster for the outlaw's single-handed hold-ups in Colorado.

There was also a substantial reward for the capture, dead or alive of Blinker Jackman. The dough was a welcome gift for all the trouble the varmints had caused. Joe figured it was only fair to share it equally with his *compadres*.

His only regret was the killing of Genesis Buckhorn. The dubious need for revenge had turned the head of this otherwise innocent victim of the Red Sash vigilantes. Joe was going make it his business to further the cause of proper law in the territories. Law that would see an end to bar-room courts presided over by despots like Zebulon Pikestaff.

'So what are you going to do now that all the fun is over?' Joe enquired of his two partners during a welcome meal at the Drovers' Kitchen.

Cactus Bob's eyes strayed to the dressmaker's shop across the street. 'Figured I might stick around here for a spell. There's plenty of work on the ranches.'

'And with a mighty fine girl to keep you company.' Joe smirked.

Bob ignored the wry comment, continuing to chew on a piece beef. His face remained devoid of expression. It was early days and he had a lot of catching up to do in the courting area.

'And what about you, Chico? Any plans?'

The Mexican shrugged. He was feeling a little deflated after all the excitement of the previous weeks and months.

'I at loose end, Señor Joe. Perhaps try luck on new gold strike in Nevada.' Although his disposition lacked the confidence needed for such an undertaking.

A measured expression formed across the scout's rugged features.

'Seems to me that with Bob here sticking around Casper, there could be an opening for an enterprising dude with De Vere Holdings in the assay office. I could ask Frisco if'n you fancy giving it a try.'

The portly guy's face lit up. He tried to express his gratitude, but it emerged as a series of spluttered grunts. Joe smiled. He'd got the message.

The group broke up soon after.

Joe headed over to the telegraph

office with the intention of sending a cable to Maggie May.

But it so happened that there was one awaiting him. His whole demeanour tingled with joy after reading that Maggie was due in Casper the following day. Now all he needed to do was tidy up the cabin so that it was fit for a lady to come a-calling.

Author's Note

The story of Derby John Daggert's epic ride to secure an alibi is no figment of the author's imagination. Such an incident did indeed occur back in seventeenth-century England. After robbing a mailcoach at Gads Hill in Kent, a highwayman by the name of William Nevison was recognized by one of his victims.

He embarked on a 200-mile journey north to York where he took part in a game of bowls. Chatting with the mayor he made a point of establishing the time of day. The ride had taken fifteen hours. When later arrested, he was able to call on the testimony of the official thus proving he was elsewhere at the time of the robbery.

The jury was convinced and Nevison was released. In those days, highway robbery was an automatic hanging offence. Charles II heard about the incident and was so impressed with Nevison's initiative that he nicknamed the perpetrator 'Swift Nick'.

This episode has always been erroneously attributed to the more famous highwayman Dick Turpin and his legendary horse Black Bess. It was the novelist Harrison Ainsworth who immortalized Turpin in order to promote his novel *Rookwood* published in 1834; a false myth that has continued to survive and grow through the years.

We do hope that you have enjoyed reading this large print book.

Did you know that all of our titles are available for purchase?

We publish a wide range of high quality large print books including:
Romances, Mysteries, Classics
General Fiction
Non Fiction and Westerns

Special interest titles available in large print are:
The Little Oxford Dictionary
Music Book, Song Book
Hymn Book, Service Book

Also available from us courtesy of Oxford University Press:
Young Readers' Dictionary
(large print edition)
Young Readers' Thesaurus
(large print edition)

For further information or a free brochure, please contact us at:
Ulverscroft Large Print Books Ltd.,
The Green, Bradgate Road, Anstey,
Leicester, LE7 7FU, England.
Tel: (00 44) **0116 236 4325**
Fax: (00 44) **0116 234 0205**

STAGECOACH TO WACO WELLS

Michael D. George

Trouble is coming, and it's due to arrive on the night train into Dodge City. Marshal Ben Carter has seen gunmen gathering at the railhead, waiting for their boss to return on the mighty locomotive speeding through the wilderness towards them. The marshal knows he is no match for the deadly men gathered like vultures. It seems like time to run or die — until bounty hunter Johnny Diamond arrives, and Carter proposes they join forces . . .

WEST OF THE BAR 10

Boyd Cassidy

A group of mysterious riders is racing along the border of the infamous Bar 10 spread, determined to fulfil one mission — the killing of Johnny Puma. With his time running out, Johnny will need to rely on more than his wits if he is to face this pack of murderous strangers and survive. It's time to accept the help of his loyal friends — the famed and dangerous riders of the Bar 10.

ARKANSAS BUSHWHACKERS

Will DuRey

Former Union soldier Charlie Jefferson
strikes up a friendship with Dave and
Henry Willis in Pottersville, Arkansas.
The brothers are planning to drive
cattle from Texas to the lumber camps
of the Arkansas timberland, and invite
Charlie to join them. But the scheme
falls foul of the Red Masks, a gang of
bushwhackers who are terrorizing the
area. To bring the criminals to justice, Charlie must throw in his lot
with the army once more . . .

TEACHER WITH A TIN STAR

Harriet Cade

Whilst studying to become a minister, Mark Brown teaches school in the little town of Barker's Crossing in Wyoming Territory. But when a local rancher begins to terrorize the nearby homesteaders, Brown knows it is time to act. For the quiet teacher has a past — he was ten years a lawman before he turned his back on that life. Now he must take up his gun one last time in defence of the helpless . . .